Dark Star

Book Five of the Immortal Kindred Series

A.D. Brazeau

The characters and events in this book are fictitious. Any similarity to real persons, living or dead, places, or events is coincidental and not intended by the author.

Dark Star
Book Five of the Immortal Kindred Series
Copyright © 2019 A.D. Brazeau
All rights reserved.

ISBN: (ebook) 978-1-949931-40-2
Print: 978-1-953335-54-8

Inkspell Publishing
207 Moonglow Circle #101
Murrells Inlet, SC 29576

Edited By Audrey Bobak
Cover art By Maria Spada

DEDICATION

For Brian and Quinn – My love for you will never
end.

A.D. BRAZEAU

CHAPTER ONE

Millicent

A cool breeze moved across the lake, water rippling as it passed. The night was quiet of all manmade sound. Buds of early spring, hanging off green branches, were ready to open any day now. This chateau was my home, the place where Jack and I would live for many years to come. Never had I been so at peace, so happy. Annecy was the perfect refuge for all of us. There was no more need to skulk about the world, lost in my heavy grief.

The charming city I chose with its close streets and waterways offered enough distraction to keep us all occupied should we tire of tranquil evenings in. Our chateau, the perfect project, was far enough away from town to provide us the seclusion we needed. This home was nearing completion as work continued around the clock to restore it to its former glory with the modern touches I required. The kitchen and bathrooms were masterpieces of the finest materials, the bedrooms and living spaces the perfect blend of old meets new.

My long melancholy was over, replaced by a joy I never dared hope for before Jack came into my life. We spent our intimate moments lost in one another, our public moments never far apart. Even now, my ginger-haired love was on the phone inside, within calling distance.

I wasn't the only one who had found their happily ever after. Annie recovered her lost love from an unimaginable torture, ending his incarceration and slipping his ring back on her finger. A secret she kept from everyone, including myself. Her joy was mirrored in my own.

Alexandre too had found love. Where that man was concerned, I still felt unsure. How could I not? Still, I was happy for him and the life he was carving out for himself. It seemed he found a woman who challenged him, exactly as he needed.

"Mills, what are you doing down there by yourself?" Annie leaned from the balcony outside the room she shared with Thayer. Her auburn locks spilled forward as her jeans and sweater-clad body bent over the railing. I loved having them here, and together, we were complete. My hope was that Annie, once a wandering soul, felt satisfied enough to stay put. We now had everything we'd ever wanted.

I shifted on my feet as I inclined my head up toward my friend. "Out for a little late-night stroll. The earth smells of endless possibilities in the spring."

"Without me? Wait right there." Annie bustled back inside, the terrace door closing with a thud, cutting off the light that a moment ago streamed outside. Busy Annie never had the time to shut doors properly. They were always slammed in her haste. This habit used to drive Alexandre crazy; I laughed to myself at the memory of his bellow sounding throughout the hall of our Savannah home as Annie burst in and out of our antique doors.

A small pang zinged in my chest. There were moments from our life in the south I missed. Alexandre and I used to while away the evenings in our beautiful living room, each of us with a book in our hand. I missed perusing the stacks of my gorgeous and over-the-top library. I missed the haunting city itself, the Riverfront, the peaceful squares,

Forsyth Park. I even missed Tess, and her luxurious little shop where Annie and I found all our treasures.

I had yet to sell the house. Instead, I left it as it was. At first, all I wanted to do was rid myself of the burden. But the house wasn't to blame for any misfortune. The more I thought about it, the more I wanted to keep it. For now, anyway. You never know what the future can hold.

I looked back over the water. The scene was not the same. A moment ago, all was still, with only the gentlest of breezes to disturb the surface. Now, the water appeared blacker, the light that shined from the stars above, somehow gone. A single cloud moved over the lake. There was a tingle in the air as if an electrical storm was brewing.

The breeze picked up and whipped around me so fast it knocked me back a pace or two, like an ocean wave. Odd. I squinted my eyes against the wind as it continued to build until I was enveloped in a frenzy of whirling air.

Was this how Dorothy felt amid the dreaded tornado? It was so fast, so strong, I was powerless against it. This type of weather was common in the Midwest of the United States, not Annecy, France. I fell to my knees, my hands grasping at the blades of grass in a futile effort to remain fixed where I was. My eyes shut tight against the assault; I couldn't see what happened. I hoped Annie wouldn't be swept away.

As quickly as it began, the wind died down. I was left shaken. I fell back on my rear end, trembling hands clearing my long hair away from my face. "What the hell was that?" I murmured.

"I beg your pardon, my lady?" a woman spoke in French somewhere behind me. The voice was familiar and didn't belong to Annie.

With my hair tucked behind my ears, I opened my eyes. This was a hallucination, it had to be. I was no longer on the grass in my backyard. The marble floor I sat on was covered in a hand-woven rug embroidered with rosebuds and vines. I remembered the day this rug was delivered. I was a new bride, still hopeful my life with my husband would be the dream I longed for. This rug had gone up in flames, along with the rest of the chateau where I lived my mortal life with Charles as his Marchioness.

The blood in my veins turned to ice water. "I must have hit my head," I whispered as I explored my scalp with the tips of my fingers. No lumps or bleeding wounds were discovered.

"My lady, you're frightening me. Are you all right?"

The voice came from my lady's maid. Her name escaped me after so long, but I was sure the high, clipped voice was hers. My heart began to thud, and a flutter of nausea wound through my stomach. I closed my eyes and pressed my fist to my chest. My heart didn't beat, it hadn't beat since...

"Please leave me." I remained as I was on the floor. Quick steps jogged to the door which opened and closed behind me. This couldn't be happening. Tears threatened to well up, but I fought them back. I wouldn't be afraid, and I wouldn't cower. There had to be an explanation for this.

I pushed myself to my feet, legs wobbly like jelly. How could I be here, in this room?

Something had pushed me back in time. As farfetched as it seemed, this was the only logical conclusion. But what? And why? This seemed like some horribly sick joke. Most terrifying of all was that I was surely human. In this state, I was vulnerable. Anything could happen. It was imperative I keep a clear head.

A loud bang on the door startled me so much I jumped a foot off the carpet. "Millicent, what is the meaning of this? You're frightening people. Are you unwell? Do I need to call for the doctor?" The voice of my mortal husband, hard and cold, sent a wave of shock through my body. So much was going on so quickly, it was hard for me to ground myself.

I remembered his fear of illness. This was something that would buy me some time. Time I dearly needed in order to get my bearings. "I'm a little sick, Charles, but there's no need for the doctor. I'll be fine if I'm left alone to rest."

Charles. Charles stood on the other side of the door. I turned to face it, disbelief whirling through my head. He was the last person I ever wanted to see again. What would I do if he pushed his way through the door? Run and hide?

"I'll have Liza come check on you, later." Liza, that was the name of my maid. Charles retreated from the door, his footfalls echoing on the marble outside. Charles wouldn't come near me if I played the sick card.

I chewed on a fingernail as I surveyed my surroundings. The room was the same as I recalled. Light glinted off the crystals of the opulent chandelier which hung over the center of the expansive space and threw dancing rainbows over the pale-rose walls hand-painted with golden birds. I loved those birds so much, I had gold hair combs fashioned in the same way. The enormous, gilded, four-poster bed sat in front of the far wall, panels of gauzy tulle floating down the sides.

I spent two years perfecting this room after I moved to the chateau. This room was my sanctuary, the one place I was able to retreat. Charles was not here often, and when he did visit, it thankfully wasn't for long. Improving the décor gave me something other than my horrendous union to focus on.

My clothes would have to be changed, and fast. I wondered if Liza had observed what I wore. She was shrewd, she would notice. Skinny jeans were not a popular clothing choice in the eighteenth century. The thought of again forcing my body into a corset made me cringe. My tight denim at least had some give. While I played sick in my room, something casual and comfortable would suffice.

I pulled off my pants and blouse, stuffing them underneath the mattress of my feather bed, and changed into a blue silk dressing gown. I would have to do something about the clothes. My life wasn't my own as Liza and the other servants were often in here cleaning and changing linens.

The terrace would be a good place to think. I padded across the floor in bare feet and cracked open a glass door. Carefully, I poked out my head. No one was around down below, so I walked all the way out, the fresh air welcome. I plopped myself onto a chair as my gaze swept the back of the property.

My breath caught in my throat. Over 250 years had passed since I'd seen the light of the sun fall over anything. Rays of bright yellow stretched out over the green of the back grass, getting lost over the hedges, and picking itself up again to play off the surface of the water in the fountain like dancing prisms of light. There was no denying the awe for such natural splendor.

Unfortunately, this wasn't my home, nor was this who I was anymore. I felt like a prisoner here. Now was no different. Chateau Mirabeau was arguably one of the most beautiful estates in France with an endless, rolling lawn, perfectly graveled paths that wound through trimmed hedges and rose bushes, and statues of Greek gods. Any woman should have been happy here. At least, that was what I was told all my mortal life. I was never happy, only listless, apathetic.

What on earth was going on? More importantly, how the hell was I supposed to get back home? I thought of Annie as she bounded out of the back door to meet me by the lake. What did she find, I wondered. Had I disappeared into thin air? I knew she would search for me. They all would.

Just when I had everything I always wanted, I was torn away, thrown back into the hated past, away from Jack. Jack. What would he do? Tears pricked at my eyes. He would be beside himself trying to find me. I could only hope he and the others were safe.

I thought about the strange wind that picked up as I turned toward the lake. It was an ominous wind, in no way natural. My musing ran to Alexandre and his demon hunting. I didn't know anything about demons. All I knew was he had fought some sort of death demon and then lost his immortality.

Alexandre was always a little too close for comfort in my mind. It stood to reason this was connected in some way. No other scenario could come close to explaining what was now happening. In what way my maker was involved, I would have to puzzle out. I could think of nothing else that made sense.

Alexandre. If I was here, why shouldn't he be? If his story was to be believed, he had built his little cabin in the woods after spying on me at my wedding. He should be there now, asleep under its very roof at this exact moment. Even if this Alexandre was the old one, he should be able to help me. He'd be able to turn me into an immortal while we figured out how to get back, so at least I wouldn't be so vulnerable. If I died here, there would never be a way to get home.

My stomach constricted. Wait. I needed to wait and be smart. Even if Alexandre was out there, would he help? At the time, he was singularly set on one thing; acquiring me. He wasn't yet the self-actualized man he'd become in the future. He'd be the old Alexandre, obsessive and terrifying.

Another thought almost caused my heart to stop. In any time-travel movie I'd ever seen, any change of events, no matter how small, could cause irreparable damage to the future. This would mean if I didn't get back, I was cursed to re-live everything as it happened more than 250 years ago.

Suddenly, I was tired, weary to my bones. If there was no way for me to get home, I would have to re-live my marriage to Charles, the affair with Julien, Julien's murder, and then my long, painful immortality with Alexandre. Not to mention, Kathryn Hart would die all over again, and Jack would have to take Alexandre's head. My own head began to spin. I didn't want to be here in the past, not when everything was perfect as it was.

I stumbled inside and crawled into the bed. If I couldn't be helped, I was in trouble. In order to make sure I would end up with Jack in Annecy, I would have to do it all over again, silent to the fact that I had already lived this life. I couldn't tell Julien, Alexandre, Annie, or Jack until I was right back in the same spot at the lake. And what was to say it wouldn't start all over again? An endless cycle of pain and torment? My head started to pound.

No, such a thing was impossible. There was no way anyone was strong enough to endure the pain I had not once, but twice. I needed to figure this out and get myself home. If I didn't, I would surely go mad.

CHAPTER TWO

Annie

Where are you, Millicent? All I could see in my mind was Mills as she stood by the lake, her smile radiant and her black eyes warm.

The days had been joyful. The four of us were very much suited to each other. Mills and Thayer shared jokes about her noble heritage and his ties to a royal family. He called her *my lady,* and she called him *Czar Thayer.* They would cackle with laughter over a jest no one thought particularly funny but them. I realized quickly how alike they were both physically and otherwise; their figures, tall and lithe, their personalities, aloof and introverted, but sweet like teddy bears when you moved past the masks of their exteriors.

Likewise, Jack and Thayer were similar in some respects, but completely different in others. Jack was also introverted, but there was no mask, only a genuine heart. He'd never needed to create a façade the way Thayer and Mills had. Thayer was stiffer, more militaristic than Jack, who was a creative, able to go with the flow in almost every circumstance.

The two men bonded over their mutual interest in

architecture as they discussed this chateau and their plans to build a mini Greek rotunda on the back of the property. The two usually silent men would talk for hours about which type of column would be most suitable. This led them into other discussions until they became quite close.

Everything was perfect. Until it wasn't.

Now, we had visitors we hoped could help in our quest to find Millicent.

"Maybe she took a powder because she's over Jack." Alexandre, now human, but still an ass, sat across from me at the pedestal table in the back of the chef's kitchen. The room was all gleaming marble and spotless chrome, a human's dream. I never understood why Mills spent so much money in here when none of us ate actual food. But she wanted the house perfect, so it would be.

The hour was late. Alexandre's pregnant fiancée, Bria, slept upstairs. That was all kinds of weird, but the only thing I could focus on now was Mills.

Thayer consoled Jack on the back terrace. The man was a wreck. He hadn't changed his clothes since the night she vanished, and his burnished hair was mussed all over from his nearly constant pulling and tugging. We all waited for the imminent arrival of Alexandre's sister, Selene, and her witch boyfriend, Tash. More weirdness.

I rolled my eyes, in no way in the mood for Alexandre's digs. "I thought you weren't jealous anymore?"

Alexandre leaned back, his arm propped on the table like he hadn't a care in the world. I knew better, though. His eyes were drawn. He was terrified we would never find her. Alexandre was as distraught as Jack, although he attempted to keep his feelings to himself. "I'm not jealous. I'm very much in love, thank you. I just don't like him."

"I probably wouldn't like someone who chopped off my head, either."

Alexandre chuckled, gazing down at his hands. "Where the hell could she be, Annie?"

All I could do was shake my head, heavy sadness hanging

around my shoulders. I wanted to change the subject, if only for a minute. "Your parentage is crazy, right? I'm kind of mad you never felt you could share it with us." My disappointment in Alexandre was nothing new. I never felt he cared much for me, only changing me at Millicent's behest so she would have another playmate.

Alexandre gazed at me, his eyes tired but warm. "I'll probably be apologizing for the rest of my life, which is going to be much shorter now. If I could go back and do things differently, I would, Annie. I was so fixated, so…"

"Obsessed," I interrupted.

"Yeah." He nodded sadly. "You received my letter?"

"I did. It was nice to read. I'm glad you've found happiness. I really am." I didn't think I could say more than that, not yet. "Alexandre, if she were…gone, do you think you'd know? Like how we knew something happened to you?"

Alexandre's brow wrinkled; his mouth turned downward. "I don't know, but I think I would."

This made me feel a little better. The thought that Mills was dead crept in and out of my thoughts. I did everything in my power to push it away. "What's it like to feel the sun on your skin, again? Tell me about it." I tried to remember the heat of the sun and how it warmed cold skin, but I couldn't.

"It's delicious. My favorite thing to do is to wake early, pour a cup of coffee, and sit on the back porch to watch the sun rise. The colors, Annie, I had forgotten the colors. The yellows, the oranges. Not only that, but the color of everything touched by the rays; the bright green of the trees and grass, the deep red of the roses. It's magnificent. I sit there until the beams bathe me in their light, until it's too bright, or until Bria yells at me from inside."

I laughed. "That's wonderful, Alexandre, truly wonderful." The scent of human blood wafted in, interrupting my train of thought. "They're here. I can smell them outside." I jumped from the table, Alexandre on my heels, and sprinted toward the door.

The witch, Tash Allerton, and his daughter were the first to arrive. Grace was young, too young to be in a room with vampires. Although she knew what we were, she wasn't fazed in the least. Her education in the bizarre must have begun early. Grace and I sat at the kitchen counter, while her dad spoke with Jack at the table behind us. Tash was a strong man, inside and out. He rivaled Alexandre in the beefy department. Tash mentioned his lineage was a long one. His line could be traced all the way back to the Salem witches of the late 1600s. An interesting story for another time, I was sure.

Selene came in not long after. I liked her immediately. This was a strong woman, with a bearing that reminded me of myself. She was a fighter. I began to feel hopeful, more hopeful than I had since Mills disappeared.

We wasted no time and gathered by the lake. Tash pulled out a map and some other witchy stuff to perform a locator spell. I had never seen this sort of thing before. Terror and excitement churned in my belly. All I could think was *find her.*

Tash performed the spell. When he said she was near her old chateau, I raced to get there. I wasn't hopeful to find her, as Jack, Thayer, and I had already looked, but I had to check. We couldn't afford to leave any stone unturned. There was nothing. When she said she'd torched the place, she wasn't kidding. One quick look at the creepy stone cabin where Alexandre stalked her also turned up zilch.

I returned and it was surmised she had been pulled through time. Selene mumbled something about an Egyptian goddess she'd summoned while in Romania who pulled Selene backward in time, leaving her nowhere to be found. Why this goddess would come after Mills was what I wanted to know. Tash's spell worked; Millicent was at the Mirabeau Chateau, all right, albeit in the late 1700s. How we would get her back was now the question. At least we knew she still lived.

Before we could get any further, something happened that I couldn't explain. A tornado-force wind blew up out of nowhere, knocking me flat onto my back. I covered my face to protect it from the dirt and debris that flew around me. I tried to yell out, to reach out for Alexandre or for Tash who sat not far from where I stopped after my jaunt to the old chateau. I worried over the mortals being picked up by the gusts and thrown into the water of the lake. I didn't have to worry long. As quickly as the gale wound up, it died down.

"You guys, seriously. What was that? Did your witchy spell go all haywire?" I sputtered out the words, bits of leaves stuck to my lips. No one answered. Everything around me was dark. "Tash? Alexandre?"

I blinked my eyes open and closed to adjust my sight. Instead of grass underneath me, I felt something soft, like a feather mattress. As my vision adjusted to the dark, I realized with a start where I was.

The subtle scent of dried cinnamon and apple skins from the chipped china bowl sitting on my windowsill brought it all back. I was in my old room at Mrs. Greaves's boarding house. I was dreaming. This was a dream. Somehow, I had been knocked unconscious, like the time Alexandre threw me against the trunk of an ancient oak tree and almost crushed my skull. My heart skipped a beat.

"What?" I pressed a hand to my breast. I breathed; my heart pounded. The room swirled around me. *Do not pass out, Annie Monroe.* Maybe this wasn't a dream, after all.

Mills was in the past, and so was I. Thoughts of what happened spiraled in my head. I couldn't grasp a single thread.

I lay flat on my back in my jeans and a t-shirt. It was a good thing I ended up in my room in what appeared to be the middle of the night. Materializing on the street in these clothes would only land me in the asylum.

Leaning up on my elbows, I attempted to think

rationally. Here I was, once again, in the eighteenth century. The thought of being human filled me with dread. I hadn't cared much for it the first time around.

Millicent was, no doubt, experiencing the same thoughts. Had I replaced the old Annie, was I the old Annie, or was there another Annie who would walk in at any moment and find me lying in her bed? I'd never traveled through time before. I tried to think about the episodes of the time travel fantasy Alexandre used to watch. I couldn't remember the name of it now as I hadn't paid much attention. Not that a fictional show would help me here.

The only thing that seemed logical was to proceed like I was the only Annie in this time. What other choice did I have? If I came face to face with myself, I'd have to roll with it.

I swung my feet over the side of the bed, human hunger gnawing at my insides. To eat solid food after all these years would be more than weird. My stomach would have to wait. If only I knew what time it was, exactly. With all the events that took place before my immortality, knowing where I was in my life was vital.

Another feeling took hold in my belly; fear. What if I did something to change the timeline? Was that possible? Oh God, I could ruin everything without even meaning to.

The room was the same. In the dark, I could see the plain but sweet furnishings, my wash basin, Mrs. Greaves's handmade quilt and the old painting of the ship caught in a storm. I used to love the depiction and would often gaze at it. I wanted to be nostalgic, but all that gurgled inside was doubt, fear, and nausea.

I stripped out of my jeans and shirt, balling them up and shoving them in the very back of my wardrobe. No one ever came into my room, so I wasn't too worried about the strange clothing being found. I threw on a nightgown and trotted down the hall to Mrs. Greaves's room. She would think I was crazy, but I didn't see that I had much choice. Sitting back to await my fate had never been my style.

The hall was dark. Silence permeated the space as my housemates slept inside the various rooms. I tried to remember who else lived here at the time. I couldn't think of anyone but Mrs. Greaves as I hadn't the time or inclination then for friends. The lady's door was unlatched, and I slipped inside.

A strange sense of déjà vu rolled through me as I watched the former mistress of the house sleep in her bed. The curtains were thrown wide, allowing the light from the full moon outside to stream into the room. She looked as she did over two hundred years ago. I suddenly felt overcome with emotion as I hovered near the door. Mrs. Greaves had been so kind to me in life, and to see her again seemed too good to be true. I wanted to throw my arms around the little woman and squeeze her. She always gave the sweetest hugs.

Benjamin. I could see my friend, again. He was here, in the same time, his home mere blocks away. It took all my willpower not to fly from the room and run through the streets. I could easily invent a reason to be at his house in the middle of the night. I was his spy, after all. To see Benjamin, to speak with him, to press his kind hand, it may break me.

First things first. It was imperative I know the exact date. To do so, I would have to wake Mrs. Greaves and let her think I had lost my grip on reality.

I crept to Mrs. Greaves's bedside, sinking to my knees alongside her. "Mrs. Greaves," I whispered. She didn't stir. "Mrs. Greaves," I repeated, grasping her shoulder.

Mrs. Greaves murmured, her eyes fluttering open. "Annie? Is something wrong?" Mrs. Greaves moved to sit up, reaching for her spectacles on the bedside table.

"No, it's fine. Please don't get up. I've had a horrible nightmare, is all. Can you tell me today's date?"

"Hmm? The date?" Mrs. Greaves's voice was thick with sleep.

"Yes, the dream was so frightening. I know it's silly, I

only need to know and then I'll leave you in peace." I crouched, nervous Mrs. Greaves would think I'd had a mental break. She surely knew I was a spy. My fear was she would think me over-stressed and report it to Benjamin, forcing him to put me on leave and alter the timeline.

"Of course, dear. It's..." She answered my question, looking at me in the dark, concern marring the usual placidity of her features.

I laughed to ease her anxiety. "That's right. Just as I thought. These dreams of mine." I patted her arm and rose to leave.

"Take care, dear," she whispered to my back. "An overburdened mind can cause more damage than you think."

"It isn't that at all, I assure you. Only a recurring childhood dream. Go back to sleep, I'm sorry I woke you." I tiptoed out the door, pulling it closed behind me. I sank back against the wall with a sigh.

In two months to the day, Benjamin would give me the assignment that would see me captured by the Hessians, and Captain Thayer Emmerich. My heart almost stopped as I thought about what this meant. I would get to fall in love with him all over again. This would seem an exciting prospect, except that I would then lose him to a cruel fate.

A little idea sprang to life in the corner of my mind. I could also save him. What would happen if I warned Benjamin about the book? What would happen if I met Thayer and told him everything that would happen? We could defeat Emilia right then and there and live together in happiness without Thayer ever having to go into that box of torture. Then, I could warn Millicent of Alexandre and assure her that if she only waits, she'll be reunited with her love.

These thoughts were interesting. But for all I knew, the very opposite could happen, no matter my good intentions. Too much could be lost if I tried to change the past.

Back in my room, I flopped on the bed as my heart

hammered away in my chest. What choice did I have but to go through with everything all over again? Thayer and I were destined to save the Culper Code Book from Emilia Romanov. After that, I would move on to Benedict Arnold and thwart his plans, sending him into permanent exile. More nausea boiled in my gut. The thought of sleeping with Benedict all over again sickened me to my core. Not only that, Thayer would again endure his centuries-long torture.

Time travel was better left to television actors. If only I had a machine to take me back. If memory served, Mills was in France, about to embark on her own journey to immortality which occurred not long before mine.

Poor Millicent would also face many hard decisions. She would see Julien, again, knowing full well what will happen to him. And, Alexandre. For a mad second, I thought to jump on a ship and head to France. It would take me so long to get there. By the time I arrived, our lives could be irrevocably altered.

Would anything really change if I did? The two months leading up to my capture were calm, and not much occurred, nothing of importance, anyway. I had the time to leave and find Mills. Perhaps the two of us working together could solve this riddle.

I tried to think of what happened right before I was swept into the past. Selene had been saying something, but what? The moment was cloudy, murky in my mind. I remembered Tash on the ground, his map spread out before him. Selene was upset...but why?

Nephthys. I was sure that was it. The Egyptian goddess of death. Selene called her forth in Romania and she was angry. This goddess pulled Selene back in time and Tash saved her. I bit my lip in concentration as I thought. This was good. At least I now had something tangible to hold on to. Tash would bring us back. Patience would be hard, nearly impossible, but that was what I had to have. What was this goddess's problem? We didn't even know her. It seemed whatever beef she had with Selene, she was extending to anyone connected with her, even if those connections were tenuous at best.

Perhaps there was even some way I could help. Why not? As I'd already established, sitting back was not my strong suit. Witches existed in this time, too. I just had to find one, then convince him or her to help me. Seemed easy enough. Selene had her witch; I could get my own. In this instance, two witches seemed better than one.

This gave me a purpose for which I was grateful. If there was anything I needed in life, it was purpose. I thought of poor Mills. She was completely in the dark about what happened. Mills had no idea there was a crazy goddess out to get us. She must be sick with worry over what she would do. If only I could call her.

My gaze shifted over to the small bureau. There were papers and ink in the top drawer. I could send her a letter. It would take weeks, but at least it was something. I had to do something, reach out to her in some way. It seemed impossible we could be here for so long. If we got back before the letter arrived, would the old Mills read it? What would she think? It seemed a harmless risk. If we were gone and the old us were put back in place, mortal Millicent would likely burn the letter as nonsense.

I tore open the drawer and brought out the writing implements. I hadn't written with a quill and ink since forever. How I longed to return to the modern time. I sat on the bed, the paper atop a book, balanced on my thigh.

Mills,

I'd like to tell you not to worry, but I'm worried, too. I'm also here, by the way, as in modern me is here in eighteenth-century Boston. The best and frustrating part is, I know why. This would sound crazy to anyone but us. Here goes; Alexandre's sister, Selene, brought forth Nephthys, the Egyptian goddess of death while she was trying to vanquish one of the horsemen of the apocalypse in Romania. Nuts, right? Anyway, the goddess was not thrilled and pulled Selene back in time as a sort of punishment. Tash, Selene's boyfriend (he's a witch btw), saved her.

After you disappeared, they came to help us locate you and we did. Only, I was pulled back, too. All this to say, there's a reason why we're here. I'm confident they will figure it out and get us back. I plan to work on an idea, as well. Try to keep to the timeline as much as possible.

P.S. If you know any witches over there, that would be helpful.
XOXO, Annie

I read back over the note, thinking how insane it all sounded. Hopefully, her awful husband didn't read her letters. He might commit her.

One question now remained for me. Where could I find myself a witch?

A.D. BRAZEAU

CHAPTER THREE

Alexandre

The bedroom was dark and cold. I shivered under the heavy down comforter. Bria, still in her first trimester, continued to be ill every day. She could only sleep if the bedroom was pitch black and freezing. She snored softly next to me; her hand clutched in mine.

I was worried for her, on top of everything else. The French doctor we saw yesterday assured us her symptoms were completely normal and both mother and baby were doing their jobs. I hadn't expressed to Bria my recurring thought; if I were immortal, I could better protect everyone I loved.

Not for one second did I regret what I gave up. I would do it again in a heartbeat. But the need to shield, not only Bria and our child, but Annie and Millicent, as well, was strong. There wasn't much I could do against the forces of evil as nothing more than a bag of bones and skin.

There was no sleeping for me tonight. Tash was set to return, my private plane landing at the local airfield, in the next thirty minutes. If he had succeeded with his coven, he should have a few friends with him.

The house would be packed. Where everyone was going to sleep was a mystery. The chateau was large, but not massive with all five bedrooms currently occupied. There were the two master bedrooms, each inhabited now by Jack and Thayer. Bria and I had a room and Tash's daughter, Grace had the room at the top of the hall, Selene, in between us. I was curious to see where Tash would sleep once he returned. Would he shack up with Selene or stay with his daughter?

These thoughts were useless. We couldn't afford to waste any time. It was my hope we all get straight to work and have my progeny home before sunrise. I wouldn't see them abandoned, nor would anyone else.

I gave Bria's hand a soft squeeze and released her to join the others downstairs. Little Grace, Tash's daughter, should also be sleeping, but a passing shadow under the door told me she crept around the hallway as she no doubt eavesdropped on the adults below. I couldn't blame her for her curiosity. I was sure she was anxious for her dad as well.

I pulled on some jeans and a sweater and tiptoed out of our room. Closing the door, I squinted my eyes to peer into the shadows of the vast second floor. "I know you're up here, miss. Didn't Selene put you to bed?"

"Selene's not my mom and I'm too old to be put to bed." The child's voice came from a darkened corner at the top of the stairs.

I bit my bottom lip to keep my snicker at bay. The girl was correct on both counts. Selene wasn't her mother, nor was she trying to be, and ten-year-olds, as far as I knew, put themselves to bed. This ten-year-old seemed more mature than most.

"Selene wants to help your dad by keeping an eye on you. We all do. There are already two women in danger, we don't need a third." It must have been hard on the kid, left alone with a houseful of undead, one sick pregnant lady, and me. Grace seemed to take the situation in stride, not too concerned by the bloodsuckers under the roof.

"I was kidnapped by one of the four horsemen of the apocalypse. I don't need anyone to keep an eye on me."

"Well, you got me there. Did I ever tell you about the time I defeated the god of death, Balor? He's a crazy-looking demon, let me tell you. He only has one leg and one eye that shoots fire like a laser beam." I stood in the hallway outside the closed door to the room I shared with Bria, my hands casually stuck in the pockets of my jeans.

A small dark head emerged into the stream of light from downstairs, dark eyes wide. Grace was an interesting girl. How many kids lived the life she did? Not many would find themselves in a French chateau with a houseful of vampires. I guessed since her dad was a witch, she wasn't too spooked by the paranormal, which was clear in her response. "No way."

"Way. I'll tell you all about it, tomorrow, if you go to bed right now."

Grace's eyes narrowed, mouth sinking into a smirk of her own. "Fine. But I want the whole story. Don't leave anything out just because I'm a kid."

"You're not my kid. I'll give you all the gory details you want."

Grace snorted a laugh, clamping a hand over her mouth to stifle the sound. She walked the five feet to the room she may or may not share with her dad, tiny bare feet padding along the wood boards, and closed the door.

I found the others in the cavernous living room. Millicent's influence was all over this house. Everywhere I looked, a pang of sadness zapped my heart. The color scheme of grays and whites flowed throughout every room with additional pops of color here and there. The extra color she had chosen for this room was a French blue. The blue and white striped wallpaper complemented both the casual overstuffed furniture and the fine, elegant details such as the crystal chandelier and the matching wall sconces.

Thayer sat on the loveseat, shoulders and head slumped forward as he read one of Selene's occult books. He wore slacks and a maroon crewneck sweater, always a little more dressed up than the rest of us. Despite this, his military bearing had given way and he appeared as broken as Jack, both men hollow about the eyes since the disappearance of the women they love.

Selene sat cross-legged on the floor, near the cold fireplace, a book spread in her lap. She wore her usual outfit of leggings and a long, silky tunic. Selene never knew Mills and she had only been in Annie's presence for ten minutes. Still, she was concerned. Her warm stare gazed up at me as I entered. "How's Bria?" she asked.

"She's asleep. Let's cross our fingers she sleeps through the night. She was able to keep her dinner down, so I'm hoping she's turned a corner. I can't imagine how miserable it's been for her." I plopped onto the sofa. Thayer glanced up at me as if I'd bothered him by sitting on a separate piece of furniture. I beamed a smile at him, the sentiment not quite making it to my eyes. What was it with Annie and Millicent and these sour saps? I got it. Thayer was freaked out, we all were.

"Fingers crossed. Pregnancy sickness is no fun, from what I can remember." Selene went back to her book but continued to talk as she scanned pages. "They should be back soon. Jack went to pick up Tash and the others, he insisted."

"Of course, he did." Do-gooder Jack couldn't help but be the first to volunteer.

Selene chuckled. From the corner of my eye, I caught Thayer glaring at me. There was no reason he should dislike me, was there? He and Jack were besties now, maybe that was the reason. Whatever. They could have each other. As soon as my progeny was home, I was out of here.

"Anyway, they should be back any minute. Tash landed early." Selene flipped another page. Her demeanor was cool and detached. I wondered if the witch wouldn't be sharing her room, after all.

I was anything but cool and detached, although I did my

best not to show it. As I thought about what lay before us, my stomach flopped a little. I was anxious to get the show on the road. Bria and I both needed to get home. I felt like an outsider here. Even if I were still immortal, I wouldn't have been welcome, probably less so.

My only concern was Annie and Millicent. Once they were returned and safe, I would take Bria and go back to Ireland. With Bria sick, the only person who spoke to me was Selene and she was busy most of the time watching over Grace. I needed banter, conversation, not moping and melancholy.

Selene was probably a little too diligent in her attention, as Grace implied upstairs. Not only had Selene not been around children in two thousand years, but she also hadn't had a serious relationship in all that time. She wanted to prove herself. I loved my sister and wanted her to be happy. I couldn't help but wonder if she could truly be happy with the witch. They didn't seem suited. But, what did I know about anything? I wouldn't have thought to find myself in love with the redhead, and I was still shocked that she loved me in return.

Headlights flashed through the front window and tires crunched the gravel of the drive. Selene and Thayer jumped up in unison, their books falling to the ground, forgotten. I remained where I was, suddenly aware that I had chewed a small hole in my bottom lip, the taste of blood metallic on my tongue.

Selene walked out into the hall to open the front door. She was out of our view. I tried to sit with patience I didn't feel. Thayer stood in front of the loveseat; his fists clenched at his sides. He seemed even less patient than I was. I hoped Tash had brought an army with him. It seemed we were going to need one to find this goddess who had my girls trapped in time.

There were murmurs in the hallway I couldn't make out. The talking seemed to go on for an eternity. When it ceased, Jack strode into the living room, dragging a trunk without too much care for the floor it passed over. Mills wouldn't be happy about that.

The man looked like a corpse, his skin paler than normal, eyes sunken, and skin sagging. It was clear to my eyes he hadn't taken sustenance since we lost her.

Jack dropped the trunk on the thick carpet with a thud, his gaze fixed on Thayer. I rolled my eyes. These two. Would they start braiding each other's hair next? After my eye roll, I noticed Jack shake his head. What that meant, I didn't know.

"What is it?" I asked Jack, dread keeping me in place.

Jack addressed himself to Thayer, not giving me the courtesy to look in my direction. "Tash wasn't able to convince his coven to help us. Not a single witch came. We're on our own."

Thayer groaned, a piteous sound for a grown man to make, and sank back on the cushions. Jack dropped his head, moving over to the mantle where he stuck out a hand to support himself as he stood.

No one came. I passed a rough hand over my face. We were on our own. My chest constricted, my throat burning as I thought of those women and what they were currently dealing with. Mills and that husband, Julien, me. Was she experiencing it all over? My heart ached. It was hard enough for her the first time around. I thought of myself all those years ago, draining her lover in that dank cellar. A chill shook my limbs.

And what of Annie? Thayer, the war, Emilia Romanov. I didn't have any love for Thayer, but to think of him lying in that box wrapped in silver chains for another two hundred years, it was cruel beyond measure. We had to get them back, no matter the cost.

Tash and Selene walked into the room hand in hand. Tash looked tired. Not quite as tired as I felt, but close. He was mortal, after all, and had traversed the Atlantic twice in the last forty-eight hours. I did have to admit his dedication to us put him in a favorable light. He didn't know any of us and he had known Selene all of a couple of weeks. I should give the witch more consideration.

Selene's free hand played with the end of her tunic as they came to a stop in the middle of the room.

"Not close with your coven, I see?" I couldn't help myself. I knew this wasn't helpful, and realized he was doing his best, but had Selene chosen the one witch on the planet who didn't have friends?

"I was, for a long time. Then, I allied myself with a horseman and became romantically involved with a vampire. All things covens discourage. I'm lucky they haven't thrown me out, yet." Tash was unperturbed by my childishness. He released Selene's hand and went to sit alongside Thayer. "As I said in the car with Jack, we're not finished. We will attempt the spell I used to get Selene back, first. I can only focus the spell on one woman at a time. So, we'll have to choose who we try for first. If it doesn't work, I can create a new spell. Most spells are ancient, and they are used for a reason. These spells have the power of our witch ancestors behind them. Creating new spells is possible, but since they are untested, they can be risky. It's a bridge we can cross when we get there. For now, we will focus on the spell I know. But—and this is important, I need to rest first."

Selene stood straight-backed and strong in front of us all. She would be the strength the rest of us required. She looked at Tash, a light in her eyes I'd never seen. "You'll go to bed right now. Sleep the rest of this night and through the day tomorrow. Will that be enough? Then we can get to work at sundown. We'll all be fresh and ready to go."

Tash sighed, his head moving up and down, but his gaze fixed on the area rug. "If it's not enough, we'll find out in a hurry."

"Okay, then. You, come with me." Selene held out her hand to a weary Tash.

He leaned forward. Before standing, he reached out to lay a hand on Thayer's arm. "I'll tell you the same thing I told Jack. Stay positive. We'll figure this out."

Thayer nodded. "I have faith," he said, his voice a half-whisper.

CHAPTER FOUR

Millicent

I awoke with a start. I must have fallen asleep. My body trembled from the nightmare, but it wasn't real, it hadn't been real. We were all in a room, everyone I loved, fighting some unseen force, and we were losing, we were losing horribly. I squeezed my eyes shut, hugging my arms around my body to still it from shaking. I could see them all so clearly, and there were others, people I didn't know. They were fighting with us. A little girl was crying, sobbing so loudly she was choking.

When next I opened my eyes, the sun was setting, the last ray of light moving along the floor. No one had come to bother me, it appeared. My stomach rumbled with hunger and I was thirsty, but not for blood.

A pitcher of drinking water sat on my bedside table. Rather than pour it into a goblet, I drank straight from the carafe. As I drank, I became even more acutely aware of how empty my belly was. Tending to my mortal body was not something I wished to bother with, but I didn't have a choice. It wouldn't do any good for me to starve to death.

I pulled the rope for Liza.

A moment later, she cautiously poked her kerchiefed head through the bedroom door. "You rang for me, my lady?" She made no attempt to move further into the room, having been terrified by Charles that I was deathly ill.

"Yes, Liza. Draw a bath and bring me some supper."

Liza looked at me quizzically, her thick eyebrows pulled together in the center.

I rubbed the back of my neck, exhaustion tense in my muscles. "Reverse that, please. Bring me supper, then draw a bath."

Liza curtsied, still half-hidden by the door. "Yes, my lady."

Once she bustled off to get my dinner, I ambled out of bed and over to the vanity. The worry that wound its way through my body was clear on my face. My eyes were bloodshot with heavy, dark bags underneath. The glass top of the vanity was littered with half a dozen crystal bottles. I rifled through them, picking each one up to pull the stopper and smell the contents. Most of them were exotic perfumes, given to me by Charles for one occasion or another. I hated every one. If I remembered correctly, I never wore a single drop, which was why each bottle was still filled to the brim.

I was no closer to a decision on what I should do. To sit and wait for something to happen was the style of the old Millicent. The woman I became after meeting Jack and fighting to the near-death with Alexandre could not lie down, hopeful that someone else would rescue her. Action would have to be taken; I just couldn't figure out what that action should be.

Liza rapped once on the door and let herself in, a tray of food balanced in one hand. She directed a cavalcade of servants who marched in with hot-water-filled copper buckets, their burdens straining in their arms. I had forgotten how primitive the times still were and would never take plumbing for granted again.

The smell of the roasted meat set my mouth watering in an instant. Liza set the tray on my writing desk, bobbed a curtsy then strode into the bathroom, eyes trained on the floor. I really had scared this tiny mouse.

Annie would fall over with laughter. As it was, I didn't feel all that sorry for little Liza. I knew that in a few months, the servants would betray me to Charles, recounting the details of my affair with Julien to him. No doubt, Liza had much to say, being that she had the most reason to be suspicious. I put this thought out of my head. It wasn't possible I would be here that long. I couldn't face it.

I tucked into the food with fervor. After demolishing the potatoes, I told myself to slow down. This was the first meal I'd eaten in over two hundred years. The last thing I wanted was to become genuinely sick. Chewing was strange. At first, it was a novel feeling, and I delighted in the taste and texture of everything. After several minutes, my jaw became tired.

Taking my time, I took small bites, picking my way through half the plate before Liza emerged. "Your bath is ready, my lady."

"Thank you, Liza," I said between mouthfuls. "Please don't return to me this evening. I need rest."

Liza bobbed up and down then left me in peace.

I pushed the plate away, my thoughts drifting back home. Jack must have been beside himself with fear. Annie was strong. She would be scared, yes, but it was Jack I really worried about. A longing to be near him ached through my body. He was my greatest love. The thought of losing that love again… No, I wouldn't let myself go down that path. This was far from over and all was not yet lost.

With my stomach full, it was time to wash up. A warm bath was the perfect place to think about what I would do next.

Everything in the room was as I remembered. My love of white marble threaded with gray veins was deeply rooted. My bare feet padded across the cold stone to the large soaking tub. Steam swirled over the surface, inviting me in. The water smelled of my favorite lavender oils. There was no window in this room and the space became warm and sultry in a hurry.

I dropped my dressing gown on the floor and stepped in. The bath was so deep that within moments, I was enveloped by heat up to my chin. It was then I remembered. I remembered the last time I sat in this bath. It was the horrible night when everything went wrong. Charles found out about Julien, his friends dragging the man I loved to the cellar while Charles dealt me a blow that would cause me to miscarry in this very spot.

I suddenly felt sick. This was punishment, indeed. Whoever brought me here did so with great malice. No longer did I wish to linger in the lovely water. Soaping up my hands, I washed as quickly as I could. It was a relief to step out.

Water dripped from my body as I wrapped a Turkish towel around myself. I took another towel to dry the wet ends of my hair as I went to my grand wardrobe. Flinging the towels aside, I threw open the doors. I'll admit that a little thrill twirled through me to behold the rich silks, brocades, satins, and feathers within. My feminine heart was full to bursting at the sight.

My fingers trailed through the expensive gowns, every color of the rainbow represented. I was here, so I may as well dress the part the times called for. Sadly, tonight was not the night for finery. This evening would require the clothing of a thief. I wouldn't be corseted, rouged, and powdered. A simple dress in a dark color was all I needed.

Every rich woman's wardrobe contained at least two gowns for mourning. I pulled forth a black satin robe a la francais without embellishment from the back recesses of the armoire. This would do perfectly. The dress would look a little deflated without a pannier, but I couldn't be bothered about such things tonight.

I slipped on a cream silk shift, delighting in the delicateness of the fabric, then the gown, making sure all the pieces were attached as they should be. I hadn't done this in a long time, and even when I wore these clothes, I never dressed myself. Getting everything just so took me longer than I would have liked.

Even casual dress at this time wasn't at all casual. Next, I pulled on a pair of black satin slippers and draped my black cape around my shoulders, dragging up the hood to cover my light-colored hair. I felt like little Red Riding Hood, only in black.

The sun was fully down. I knew Alexandre would be up, stalking around his cabin. Perhaps he was watching me now and knew I was coming for him. I wasn't sure about this, by any means. Alexandre as he was at this time, terrified me to the tips of my toes. There was no reason for him to believe me and even less reason for him to help me. What choice did I have? I wasn't going to sit around and wait for Charles to visit me in the middle of the night. That thought terrified me more than anything else.

Escaping the house would be difficult. It was supper time, so Charles and most of the servants should be in and around the dining hall, or below stairs serving their master.

The door to my bedroom opened without a sound. I stuck out my head, craning to see left and right. There was no one about. I swept out, gathering my skirts in one hand and pulling the door closed with the other. Pants and boots would be so much more practical. The rustling of my skirts was louder than what made me comfortable.

My stomach dropped as a thought occurred to me. The hallway was aglow with lit candles tucked into sconces, but the woods would be different. My preternatural eyesight was gone. I didn't have a lantern or any means to see in the dark as I traversed the forest. Damn. I didn't have the time to mess around and look for the implements I would need. I would have to go for it and hope I didn't break an ankle.

The hallway was silent as I made my way toward the winding, marble staircase. I gripped the burnished railing in both hands, my gaze sweeping the foyer below. I couldn't believe my luck, it was deserted. Bunching up my skirt, I took the stairs one at a time, my tiptoes clacking on the stone steps and echoing with more intensity than I would have liked.

I continued down the spiral, tension roping around my neck. When the front door was in sight, I began to breathe. *Almost there.* I took a firmer hold of my skirt.

Three steps from the bottom, the butler, an overstuffed man of small stature, startled me by walking out of the darkened parlor to my left.

The breath caught in my throat so forcefully, I almost choked. I pressed my body into a shadow created by the curve of the staircase, my heart hammering in my chest with such force I thought I might throw up. If he saw me, what would I say? I was sick and needed air seemed a good ploy, but he would no doubt tell Charles I was out of bed. I wasn't ready to deal with him.

The butler walked on, oblivious to my presence. When he passed out of the foyer and into the great hall, presumably on his way to the dining room, I sucked in a great breath of air and bolted for the door. It was now or never.

Somehow, I made it outside. All the air I held within exploded from my lips in a great gush. I stood on the stone porch, the vastness of the chateau stretching out to both sides.

How impressive this building was to me the first time I laid eyes on it. Charles was a rich man, and my father was beyond pleased to hand me off to such a nobleman, a man who would save my father from ruin and elevate us both to the height of French aristocracy.

I remembered the first day I arrived here. After stepping from the carriage, not on the arm of my new husband, but the arm of the footman, my gaze swept the creamy stone of the chateau. I stood still as I counted the number of windows. When I got to thirty, I stopped. Chateau Mirabeau was among the finest in all of France, and I hated it. I hated it before I ever even stepped inside. I had done enough time here.

My skirts still in one hand, I took off at a dead run for the woods. Whether anyone saw me or not became secondary. I had to get away from this nightmare. There was enough light from the sky to see without much difficulty. I knew this would change once I was under the cover of the dense forest trees.

All I had to rely on was a long-ago memory of the path, the path laid out for me by Alexandre. I found the way easily. Funny how one recalled such things.

The small opening was exactly where I remembered, a fan of leaves obscuring it enough to keep it hidden from anyone else. Not that anyone here would be poking about in the woods. I closed my mind to old remembrances and plunged ahead.

Darkness enveloped me the moment I stepped through the leaves. I stood for a moment to get my bearings. This was risky in more ways than one. Not only was I upsetting the timeline, but I was also throwing myself at a vampire who would go on to kill Julien and then Kathryn Hart, all due to his obsession with me. Yes, he would change, presumably change, but the man I knew was ahead of me would only have one goal; to make me his dark bride.

I dropped my skirts, bringing my hands to my neck to massage the rigid muscles. This situation was unprecedented. I needed help from someone powerful. Alexandre was that person for me. If I couldn't make him see reason, I would flee back to the chateau. But this wouldn't happen. I was sure I could make him do what I wished. How strange it was that I was more confident in my ability to control Alexandre than in my ability to control Charles.

With my eyes firmly on the ground, I picked my way down the path, further and further into the forest. The road was well-cleared, and not a stone or stick lay in my way. There was nothing to fall over if I kept to the center. The forest was cool and calm. There wasn't the slightest breeze to disrupt the leaves. The scent of earth was sharp.

After losing track of how far I'd gone, the path gave way to a clearing. At the center of the clearing was the cabin, as it was the night I came here in desperation. The assault on my senses was profound. It was like moving from one moment of déjà vu to another. I closed my eyes, my feet swaying a bit underneath me.

The small, rounded door swung wide. There he was. My breath all but stopped. Alexandre, dressed as a peasant in a loose white tunic over beige pants, stood with one hand on the open door and the other stretched out toward me. Here he was, the Jupiter from my dreams who became my maker, my friend, my lover, and almost my killer.

I admit, I wanted to run to him, to allow him to take me in his arms as he did the night my world turned upside down. I knew he would hold me tight, keep away everything that scared me. But I resisted. This me knew better than to trust him so blindly.

I walked forward, my gaze locked with his. Those baby blue eyes, like an endless sea, beckoning me forward. He appeared so rakish with his mop of blonde hair falling over one eyebrow, his superhero muscles flexing beneath the soft fabric of his clothes. I laughed.

Alexandre narrowed his eyes, his grin wide and wicked. "What's so amusing, my love?"

"You. But that's a story for another time."

My maker couldn't have looked more perplexed. Alexandre was speechless. He continued to hold out his hand. I moved up the little steps but didn't take it. No matter what, I would have to resist Alexandre's charms.

"May I come in? We have a lot to talk about."

CHAPTER FIVE

Annie

Salem was where I was headed. After wracking my brain for the better part of an hour, I decided it was better than doing nothing. There was no guarantee I would find what I needed, only a way to expend the nervous energy that twitched in my limbs.

It was still dark, perfect for someone who didn't want to encounter anyone she knew.

I pulled on my old navy damask gown and covered it with a black cloak. This dress had been much worn, and I remembered how fun it was to wear all the new silks and satins Millicent bought for me after the change.

After tiptoeing my way out of the boarding house, I jogged two blocks to the stables. My lungs burned with the effort, but there was no slowing down.

The cobblestone streets of Boston were slick with moisture from the evening mist that hung over the trees and buildings. The mist dulled the light from the streetlamps, creating a creepy effect. I imagined a fiendish killer snatching young women from the street to butcher them in the shadows. Chills swept down my back. *That's London, not*

Boston, Annie.

As it was the middle of the night, the big, sliding door of the stable was locked up tight. I remembered the man who ran the place was thin-haired and wide-bellied. His name was Jim something. I rattled the wood back and forth, attempting to knock the bolt loose.

"Just what do you think you're doing, miss?" I jumped, my hand hitting the old boards and drawing a large splinter. I sucked in a breath as I gripped my injured hand in the other.

Spinning around, I saw the proprietor before me, small hands placed on large hips. "Oh, Jim. You scared me. I'm sorry to have disturbed you, but I'm in a terrible hurry and need to procure a horse for a few days. Do you have one?"

Jim pulled a face full of male judgment. "A young lady shouldn't be traipsing around in the middle of the night, alone. Just what do you need a horse for?"

I didn't have time to get into female independence, so I went with an excuse I used often at the time. "My aunt has been taken ill; I've received a note from her. It's imperative I get there quickly so I can care for her." *Isn't that what we women do, Jim? Take care of others?*

Jim seemed to consider this, looking me up and down to size up the truthfulness of my story. For a moment, I was bitter that I had to give a reason at all. I batted my stupid eyelashes and smiled brightly.

"All right. You have money?"

"Of course." I pulled a handful of coins from my pocket and Jim's demeanor changed. He pocketed the cash then unlocked the heavy door.

"You can take the dappled mare at the end." He moved ahead of me, pulling a saddle from a shelf and lugging it down the length of the stable.

Grateful to be out of Jim's line of sight, I took off with the mare at a trot. Her name was Demeter, a good name and a surprising one. Salem was about four hours away. If

Demeter and I kept a good pace, we would be there as the sun was rising. It would be a long night.

Keeping my eyes open became increasingly difficult. I was human now and needed the rest. There would be time for everything my body craved as soon as I made it back home. My thoughts had previously centered on Mills and what she faced over in France. Now, all I could see in my mind's eye was Thayer.

I hadn't spent so long without him to lose him all over again. Whatever it took, I would make my way back. My strong soldier was beside himself with worry. There was no need to speculate as to what he was feeling. I knew. I imagined him standing straight, always at attention, but with his heart breaking inside his chest. Mine was breaking, too. I was not a sentimental person in most regards, but there were two people I wouldn't be able to live without. One was stranded as I was, and one was so far away, I feared I could never reach him. This was exactly why I required action.

My human body gave me more trouble than I expected. By the time I reached the outskirts of Salem, my behind was so sore I didn't think I would be able to walk without limping for the better part of an hour. My limbs were so heavy with fatigue, all I wanted to do was curl up in a ball and sleep.

Demeter and I clopped into town over the brick road. There were already a couple of souls about as the sun began to rise. *The sun.* I pulled the horse to a stop, turning my face toward the east. I could make out a sliver of light ascending over the horizon, peeking through the bank of trees. Reds and yellows exploded over everything in its path the higher the sun crept up. It would have been lovely to watch, but I had to move on.

Demeter and I ambled further into town, passing a small white, steepled church. The smell of fresh bread, baking nearby, wafted in the air, setting my stomach to rumbling. I stopped the horse, sliding off her to pull her after me as I walked.

I would have to be discerning to find what I sought. It was the 1700s. I couldn't walk up to someone and casually ask if they knew any witches. This wasn't 1600s Salem, but they'd probably still lock me up.

The village was small with close streets and stone buildings that seemed to loom above me at crooked angles. I found a stable off a side street where I was able to leave Demeter while I explored.

My first stop was the bakery. My mouth watered as I peered inside. Fresh biscuits, muffins, and loaves of bread sat in the window. My stomach was as empty as it could be, and a loud groan ripped through me. A red-faced lady in a lace cap was pulling her goods from a basket to fill up the display. I eagerly crossed the threshold.

"Good morning," I said to the woman.

"Morning, love. What would you like?" The lady baker turned toward me, her hand hovering over her goods.

"A muffin, please."

She twisted herself back to her window, pulling out a muffin and passing it to me. In exchange, I handed her a small coin. "Let me get your change." The woman puffed her way to a counter at the back of the room.

"No need. Please keep it." I picked at the muffin, tearing off a fluffy piece and popping it in my mouth. It was still warm and melted on my tongue. "Maybe you could help me with something. I'm looking for someone who can assist me with an ailment."

"You want Dr. Coates. His house is right at the far edge of town." She pointed toward a wall, which I believed meant north.

"No, not a doctor. I'd like someone who…" I tried to think of how to ask for a person who works in alternative medicine. "Herbs. Someone who works with herbs. Do you know of anyone like that in Salem?"

The woman's face turned to stone. She looked down, plunking my coin into a box. "Don't know what you're on about. Good day to you, miss."

I'd been dismissed. No matter, I could find what I needed on my own.

I kept my eyes and ears open as I resumed my walk up the street. If there were witches here, maybe they would be attempting to blend in. But how? After walking for a few minutes, I came across a low hanging sign that read *Herbalist.* This was promising. Why had the woman at the bakery not sent me here? I shook my head, chuckling to myself at the prejudice.

The establishment was made of an unassuming white-washed stone. A heavy, wooden door was shut to the world. Before entering, I gazed around. A man across the way swept the stoop of a pub, the door thrown open to the outside world. Even the business next door, *Fabrics and Finery*, had thrown open its windows and door.

The *Herbalist* appeared alone, shut up tight against those who would intrude. I gripped the handle, turned it, and pushed the door open. A pungent earthy odor blasted me in the face. I screwed up my nose and stepped over the threshold, pulling the door closed behind me.

The space was dark. A lantern was lit in a back room, barely visible through a low-hanging archway behind the counter. From this light, I could make out through the dusty murk a crowd of shelves all packed with glass jars of various sizes. The jars were filled to varying degrees of fullness with dried herbs, flowers, and roots. Each jar was smudged with dirt and dust. A large black spider spun its web between the *Thyme* and *Wolfsbane*.

I walked around the small room, the hem of my skirt dragging in the dirt of the floor. There was a heaviness to the air that didn't feel quite natural as if this shop were not in a small Massachusetts village, but a more tropical location where humidity smothered the breath.

"What do you need, girl?" The voice came out of nowhere with not a sound to announce its arrival.

My heart stuttered a few beats as I spun around. Two feet away from me stood a woman whose age was impossible to guess. If pressed, I would say mid-forties, but she could have easily been twenty-five or even sixty-five. Her hair was a light strawberry-blonde and fell straight down to her waist. She wore the clothing of a man; breeches and an untucked white shirt, open at the collar. Her feet were bare. The sight of the woman took me aback. I wondered if I had made a mistake coming here, but it was too late to backtrack.

"Good morning, I…" Words failed me. What was I supposed to ask for? *I'm looking for a witch who can help me,* suddenly seemed ridiculous. Yet, what else was there to say?

The woman lowered her head, her gaze locked with mine in a way I found almost mesmerizing. "You're lost. You need help," she whispered.

My head bobbed up and down. "Yes. Only I'm not sure how to ask for what I need."

Her mouth ticked up at the corners in a smile that was more of a sneer. "Ask, and you shall receive."

I swallowed, a little bile rising to the back of my throat. "I'm looking for a witch." After the word fell from my lips, my head darted around my shoulders, fearful someone else may hear me.

She laughed, not a cackle as I would have expected, but a soft demure laugh like that of a fine lady. "I know. Come with me."

The woman turned on her bare heel, disappearing into the back room. I stood for a moment, unsure whether I should bolt out the door or follow. If I ran, I would never get out of this time. Taking a deep breath, I followed the strange lady. I tried to tell myself I had been in more frightening places than this.

Bare floors gave way to unfinished wooden planks as I moved into what appeared to be a living space. There was a stove emanating a steady, warm heat at the far end. Two lanterns hung from a beam in the center of the room, casting a fair amount of light. The space was tidy but bare. There was no love in the décor. The woman sat at a small, plain table, a wooden chair pulled out, I presumed for me.

I sat across from her, my spy eyes taking note of all points of entry and exit. Besides the way we came in, the only other way out was directly behind the witch and into what appeared to be the kitchen. Who knew if there was an exit from there. From where I sat, I saw the dark outline of a larder and a cooking stove.

"Do you live here alone?" There were no indications of other life; no shoes, toys, or sounds of any kind.

"That's not what you want to know." She sat with her hands folded on the top of the table, her eyes penetrating mine. Her affect was flat. I couldn't get a read on her if I tried.

"Fine. Are you a witch or not? I need a real one, not someone who fancies herself different from the pack."

"I'm who you need. But what do I get in return? You don't expect me to work for free, do you? I have to maintain all this somehow." She raised an eyebrow and threw out a hand to emphasize her point. This woman was dangerous. An unsurety of the position I held in space surrounded me as if I may fall through the floor at any time. Tension pricked at the back of my arms. I should get her together with Emilia Romanov. They would have a lot to talk about.

"If you get me back to my friends…" I stopped in mid-sentence. If this were present day, I'd be able to offer her a vast amount of money. As it was, I didn't have much. "Actually, I'm not sure. I'm very wealthy in my time, but that's hundreds of years from now."

"There are other things besides money, Annie. You have many gifts to offer."

My skin crawled as she looked me over. "How do you know my name?"

She ignored the question, her roving gaze stopping at my eyes. "A tooth, for example. You wouldn't miss one little tooth."

My stomach bubbled, waves of nausea rolling through me. Chills raised the fine hairs on the back of my neck as my hand shot to my mouth. "What the hell do you want with one of my teeth?"

"Testy. Watch your tone with me, girl. That's my business. Do you want my help, or don't you?"

I squirmed, moisture beading along my hairline. The room was stifling. "What else can I give you?"

"There are other things. If you'd prefer, we can come to an agreement on payment at another time." Her expression was hard to read. She hid her emotions well.

Bargaining with a witch didn't seem in my best interest, no matter what she asked of me in return. She could easily trick me by saying all she wanted was a lock of hair, when in truth she was taking a piece of my soul, or my ability to love. I turned in my chair with every intention of standing up and abandoning this whole stupid idea. She could take anything from me in exchange for her services. I held no power here.

A thought came to me. Maybe the name would mean something to her. It was worth a shot. "In the future, a friend is helping me. A friend with ties to Salem witches. His name is Tash Allerton."

The woman narrowed her eyes, leaning forward in the chair. I met her hard stare with my own. She had reacted. I knew when I had someone on the hook and this witch was on my hook. All I needed to do was reel her in. "That name means something to you, doesn't it?"

She leaned back, her eyes softer. "My name is Abigail Allerton."

CHAPTER SIX

Alexandre

Tash was exhausted from his trip to Baton Rouge. He went to bed immediately after giving the rest of the bad news; we were alone. I drifted in and out on the sofa in the living room. I was restless and disturbing Bria was the last thing I wanted to do. Besides, I didn't want to miss a thing.

Jack had disappeared, which was fine by me. Thayer and Selene sat in the same spots they occupied earlier, heads bent over Selene's volumes. "Do you really think you'll find anything that we can use in those books?" I was surly, massaging the back of my neck while I lay on my side, facing my sister.

"It's better than doing nothing." Selene continued flipping pages, not bothering to look up.

"We need to get on with it, Tash can rest later. Getting them home is imperative." I rolled onto my back, eyes trained on the ceiling. If Selene was implying I wasn't helping, I got the message loud and clear. I was as useless as a wet rag, another reason to choose immortality.

"We are all aware how urgent the situation is, Alexandre. Tash won't do either of them any good if he isn't at one hundred percent. There are too many things that could go wrong on the best day."

Thayer lifted his head from his book, his gaze striking me like lightning. "Your comments are unnecessary. If you wish to be of help, do something rather than sleep." The soldier's attention snapped back to scanning the page. Thayer didn't have much to say, but when he did speak, he made sense. If he wasn't so close with Jack, I may have liked him.

"Toss me something, Selene." I grunted, pushing myself into a sitting position.

Selene picked up a leather-bound tome and handed it toward me. "I'm not throwing these. Some of these volumes are older than I am."

The book was well-worn, the smell of the leather deep. The cover was etched with two stars and a waxing crescent moon. I remembered this text from Ireland. Its pages were filled with the mystical powers of the heavens.

"What do you know about tarot cards, Alexandre?" Selene surprised me by speaking when I thought we were finished with conversation for the time being.

"Probably less than you, why?"

Selene looked at Thayer, who shook his head. "I'm not sure, maybe nothing."

"It isn't nothing or you wouldn't have brought it up. Spill." I closed the book, setting it in my lap to hear Selene's story.

She shrugged, mouth turning in a frown. "When we were in Brasov, Tash left me tarot cards as a warning. That's all a long story. We can get into it later. To expedite the process, he took me to a psychic for a tarot reading."

I was trying my best to follow but knew very little about what had occurred in Brasov. Guilt welled inside me as I realized I hadn't even asked her how it went. I knew nothing of how she met Tash or how much danger she had been in, being too occupied with my fear over Mills.

"I'm sorry, Selene. Do you want to talk about what

happened? I feel like an ass for not even asking."

She shook her head. "It's okay, Alexandre. There's a lot going on here. I'll fill you in later. Suffice it to say we were successful. What I'm thinking about right now are the cards."

I nodded, indicating she should go on.

"The psychic, really interesting lady, by the way, read my past, present, and future. At the time, I thought the future she read was the future where I vanquished War, but now I'm wondering if the future she read is this future. Are you following?"

Thayer leaned forward, engrossed by Selene's words. "Did you say War? As in the Four Horsemen of the Apocalypse, War?"

"I did, and I'll tell you guys all about it, but the cards, what do you think?"

I was as intrigued as Thayer, also on the edge of my seat. "What were the cards?"

"There were seven of them; The Empress, which means motherhood. The Nine of Swords, hopelessness, Seven of Pentacles, diligence, Nine of Wands in reverse, exhaustion, Ten of Swords, failure, The Hanged Man, sacrifice, and Death, which means change." After listing her tarot spread, Selene did something I'd never seen her do before, she chewed on her lip.

I looked at Thayer, who sat unmoving, his eyes trained on the ground. Like I had said, I knew nothing about tarot cards, but those sounded awful, except for the first one. I swallowed the knot forming in the back of my throat. "Well, the motherhood card, that one's obvious, right? It means the inclusion of Grace in your life."

Selene nodded, smoothing a hand over her hair. "That was my thought."

My hopes deflated. "Diligence sounds okay, but hopelessness, exhaustion, failure, sacrifice, and change do not. I, for one, am sick of sacrifice. Can Tash read your cards again? Or maybe mine?"

"I don't know, Alexandre. I'm not sure what good it would do. Both the psychic and Tash said that the future is not fixed, we can change it at any time by choosing a different path."

"What's the point then? How do we know which is the correct path?" To say I was frustrated at this moment would have been an understatement.

Selene laughed softly. I didn't think the situation was funny and scrunched up my face. "I'm sorry, Alexandre. It's just that I said the same thing."

No one spoke after that. There didn't seem to be more to say. I wanted to further express my disdain in witches and psychics but that didn't seem helpful, so I went back to the book. The peace was short-lived.

From the corner of my eye, I watched Jack enter the room. He crossed in front of Selene, careful not to step on her precious books, and sat lightly next to Thayer. Why couldn't he disappear? I'd happily swap him for either of the girls. Maybe he could be the one to offer the sacrifice this time.

I had every intention of fixing my attention on reading. Instead, Jack leaned forward, his elbows propped on his knees. I glanced at him. Jack was staring at me, hard.

"Is there something I can do for you?" I drawled, annoyed with my frail humanness in the face of a vampire who would love to see me fully broken. He knew I wished the same for him.

Jack's mouth was a hard line, his eyes narrowed with hate. "I can't help but think this would have never happened if we had killed you properly."

Thayer snapped his book shut, his back straightening as he sat alongside his friend. He didn't speak, but his eyes went wide, and his senses were on high alert. The man reminded me of a German Shepherd. I'd no doubt Thayer would take Jack's side if it came to a fight.

Selene sighed. "Boys, this isn't the time. If you want to blame someone, you can blame me. I'm the reason this is happening, not Alexandre. It's my fault she's awake. It's my fault she took Annie and Millicent."

Jack's scowl deepened, his eyes never leaving mine. His blue eyes were several shades darker than mine, and there was a storm brewing behind them like an ocean swell. "What I can't understand is why this goddess chose them in the first place. Why not take Alexandre or one of us? Why not take you, again, since you're the one she's angry with?" Jack shot Selene a threatening look.

My sister kept her cool, her face soft and understanding. "I don't know. She felt I was an abomination. In a way, it makes sense that she would go after other vampires. Alexandre is human now. Millicent and Annie are connected to me through him, albeit loosely. Nephthys isn't exactly stable, so her decisions don't necessarily have to have any rhyme or reason. I know you're scared, Jack. I'm so sorry. The one thing I can promise is we will do whatever we can to get them both home to the men who love them."

Jack and Thayer retreated to another room with an armful of books and one last dirty look thrown my way from Jack. I slumped back against the cushions, my hot air deflated and released.

"He's hurting, Alexandre." Selene had yet to move a muscle. She sat in preternatural stillness, her legs crossed, her voice soothing. It must be nice to be so unperturbed.

"So am I." I stared at the round, marble-topped coffee table piled with art books. Millicent loved marble, placing the stone everywhere she could. Jack could spend three lifetimes with her; he would never know her as I did. "The thing is, I get it. If I'd had the good sense to die, the girls would be safe."

"Stop calling them girls, it's creepy. They're strong women, and they'll be fine. The only danger they face is reliving their lives, which can't be all that bad. They made it this far, didn't they? I truly believe we can get them back, but it could be worse. And if you had died, you wouldn't have defeated the threat of Balor and fallen in love with Bria. I hope you're not forgetting about her in all of this."

I bristled. "Of course, not. Bria's the love of my life. But so was Millicent, at one time, and Annie, Annie is just as special. It's complicated."

"I know it is. I can sympathize, have patience."

To have patience was easier said than done. The sooner Tash woke and started stirring his cauldron, the better. But, with dawn approaching, I knew I was in for a long day. There was no way Tash would begin until the vamps were awake, meaning we couldn't get started until the sun went down.

Selene propelled herself to her feet in one liquid motion. As she stacked her books on the table, she glanced up at me. "I'm going to go to bed. I wish you would do the same. You don't look well, Alexandre. We all need to be at our best."

"Maybe…" An idea, dark and unbidden, came to mind, but I pushed it away.

"Maybe, what?" Selene prodded.

I looked away, my thoughts swirling like a mosaic. "No, I couldn't do that to Bria."

Selene crossed her arms, hovering over me like a schoolteacher. "You want your immortality back." It was a statement, not a question.

My shoulders moved up and down in a sigh. "I do and I don't. This feeling of weakness, of vulnerability, I hate it. To be strong and fearless again would help me feel a lot better. I'd be a lot more confident in a scuffle with Jack the ginger. On the other hand, Bria would never consider joining me, and I couldn't hurt her like that."

"I understand how torn you must feel. You were immortal for a long time. I imagine it's hard to cast off. I love Bria and I love you. If you decide you absolutely must have it back, I'll give it to you."

My gaze swept toward my sister. "Thank you, Selene." I wanted to say more, but emotion welled up in my throat and I couldn't have that. It was swallowed down as I stood to accompany her upstairs. Never had someone been so fully on my side as my sister. Bria was my love, my partner, but I hadn't expected such a feeling of loss when I became human. I thought I would get used to it, and maybe I still would. Only a few weeks had passed, and I had been a blood sucker for a long time.

I left Selene outside her door to move toward mine. As soon as I was inside, I stripped down, the usual way I slept, and slid into the warm bed next to my sleeping Bria. She stirred. As she rolled over to face me, pushing her red mane out of the way with long, elegant fingers, she opened her eyes, fixing me in an intense stare.

"What's new downstairs?"

"Tash is back. I guess we get to work at sunset."

Bria murmured something that sounded like, "Good," and pushed herself against me. Her breath tickled my neck as I wrapped my arms around her. What was I thinking? There was nowhere I would rather be than by this woman's side. Yes, I hated my human body, but I loved Bria with every beat of my heart. She meant more than the power I lost. I'd just have to find another way to beat Jack into a pulp.

"You know, I'm feeling much better." Bria's voice couldn't have been sexier as she breathed into my chest. She nipped playfully at my pec, her hand trailing down my stomach.

I sucked in my breath as her hand moved lower. "You sure? Don't want you to throw up on me."

Bria sank her teeth further into my chest, not so playful this time.

"Ouch. I guess you asked for it."

Bria giggled as I flipped her onto her back. It was good to hear her laugh after weeks of illness. I hoped this meant she was turning a corner and wouldn't be miserable for the duration of the pregnancy.

We kissed like we hadn't kissed in weeks, which we hadn't. Moving on top of her firm body was heaven. Her moans were a delight to my ears. All I wanted was her pleasure, her happiness.

I trailed my tongue down her neck to drop kisses along her defined clavicle, one of my favorite parts of her body. Pushing up her t-shirt, I ran the tips of my fingers along the edges of her breast, playing with her until she was panting beneath me. I took hold more firmly, moving my thumb over her taut nipple.

Before I could move lower, Bria took a handful of hair and tugged. "Let's get to the good stuff. It's been too long," she breathed.

I brought my mouth back to hers and moved my hand between us to sweep aside the small swath of cotton between her legs. She was more than ready. The second I plunged into her, Bria arched her back and enveloped me in her arms. This was my home.

At sunset, we gathered in the kitchen, waiting for Tash to tell us the plan. A strange crew we were. Bria was up, sitting at the kitchen table with Grace and Selene. It was wonderful to see her color restored as she tucked into a piece of toast and giggled at some quiet joke she shared with the little girl.

Thayer, as usual, held up the wall. I couldn't imagine what the wall would do without him there. Jack sat on a stool at the bar, his eyes glued to Tash, who stood at the island, all manner of paraphernalia spread out before him alongside an old, beat-up metal box.

I stood opposite Tash, my hands shoved into the pockets of my jeans, attempting to avoid Jack's eyes at all costs. He could hate me all he wanted. My goal was to get the women, not girls, back here where they belonged, so I could get home to Ireland with Bria, where I belonged.

After several minutes of awkward silence, it was little Grace who finally spoke. "So, Dad. Are you going to tell everyone what's up or keep staring at your stuff?" I liked this girl more and more all the time. She and Bria giggled, again, two peas in a pod.

Tash continued staring at his spread of odd trinkets, his head bobbing up and down in a yes. He took a deep breath, then looked toward Grace with a smile. "Gathering my thoughts, sweetie." Tash turned his attention to Selene. "This is going to be complicated. I will basically be performing three different spells at once; a locator spell, a binding spell, and then a spell to pull them forward through time. This will not be easy."

I shifted on my feet. "You said that already."

"Alexandre." Bria frowned, shaking her head from side to side. I scowled but kept my mouth shut.

Jack leaned forward, his hands working themselves nervously on the bar top. "Why do you need the locator spell? Don't we know where they are? Millicent's in Burgundy."

"I will need a more precise location, nothing vague. We know Annie is likely to be in Boston, but even in the 1700s, that's a lot of area. It must be narrowed down in order to get a good lock on her. Instead of maps of the world, I've brought a map of France and a map of Massachusetts. After we know exactly where they are, my plan is to use a binding spell. With this, I'll bind each woman's life force to my own before I attempt to move them through time."

"Bind your life force? I don't know if I like the sound of that." Selene spoke from her chair, the wood creaking as she pushed it back.

"Me, either," echoed Grace.

"I think the spell will be more effective that way and, in the end, safer for everyone. When I pulled you back, Selene, I didn't think to do this, as I didn't have time to move through the spells properly. You could have slipped away from me and ended up somewhere else entirely."

Selene nodded, her gaze sliding toward Grace. Out of all of us, Grace seemed the most stoic, her head held high, her back straight.

"And there's another thing." Tash's gaze flicked

between Jack and Thayer. "I think I should only pull them one at a time. Once we have one of them back, I'll have to rest and reset. Then, we can try for the other."

I stepped forward, ready to take charge of this situation. "That's easy. Millicent first."

Thayer shoved himself away from the wall, his eyebrows pinched together. "Why not Annie first?"

I looked at Jack, who glanced at me before sliding off the stool. He moved toward Thayer, his hands down at his sides. "Millicent is in the most danger. I think Annie would agree."

"No, she isn't. What does Millicent have to contend with, a hateful husband? Annie is fighting a war. She's contending with people who would take her life."

Jack shook his head. "I don't think any of us really knows how this works. It stands to reason that if they do everything the same, the outcome of their lives won't change. We know they both make it safely through that time, only Millicent's was the most traumatizing. To make her re-live it all is cruel. She needs to be first."

Thayer slumped back against the wall. "Do you really think they are retracing their steps exactly? I seriously doubt Annie is. If I know her, and I do, she's doing everything in her power to get back here, timeline be damned, which is why she should come first."

Selene stood up from the table, her chair screeching across the tile. "What do any of us know about time travel? This is a serious question." Selene looked at each of us in turn, receiving only blank looks for answers. "Okay, not much. Nothing's changed here. We are all as we were, so if they are deviating, so far, their choices haven't changed the future. If they're smart, I don't think it's a concern. The other thing to consider is that this was meant to happen all along, meaning that they were always fated to go back."

I pushed a hand through my hair as I thought through what Selene was saying. "I don't believe in fate. Besides, if they were always meant to time travel, wouldn't they remember? Or, wouldn't there be a double of them in the past that they would have to avoid?"

"You guys are making my brain want to explode. I'm going upstairs to watch TV." Grace hopped down from her chair and strode past us one by one without making eye contact.

"My brain's also about to explode," I said.

Tash moved some of his trinkets around, his brow wrinkled in concentration. "I think what we're getting at here is none of us has any idea how time travel works or how a time traveler should behave. The important thing to focus on is getting the women home. To make it fair, we'll flip a coin. Jack, Thayer, are you in agreement?" The two men looked at each other and nodded.

"A coin? I agree with Jack, shocking, I know, but Mills needs to come back first." Although I hadn't said so, I was with Jack the moment he spoke for Millicent.

Tash disregarded what I said. He pulled a quarter from his pocket. "Selene call it for Annie."

Selene slid her gaze toward Tash. She was the neutral party, so it made sense for her to be in control. "Heads."

Tash set the quarter on his thumb and flipped it into the air. He caught it in his other hand. Without looking, Tash slapped the quarter into his palm and looked down. "Heads. Annie is first."

CHAPTER SEVEN

Millicent

The inside of the cabin was exactly as I remembered. A shudder ran through me as I thought back to that night, so long ago. After finally finding the love I'd always dreamed of, it was all lost in a matter of minutes, along with the child I carried. This cabin was a refuge during the darkest night of my life.

I moved around the compact space, my gaze falling onto the bed where Alexandre would work the change. He stood behind me, the door to the outside world closed behind him.

"Millicent, I'm so happy you came to me. I must admit, I did not think you would come for a while yet." Alexandre's voice was strong. It carried throughout the room, moving around me with memories I didn't want.

With my back still turned on him, I sat at the wooden table in a rustle of silks. "Sit down, Alexandre, please. I don't have a lot of time and there is much to impart. What I have to say will be hard for you to believe, but you must. There is no one else I can turn to."

"You've learned my name? It's not Jupiter anymore.

How?" Alexandre crossed the room in three large strides, pulling out a chair opposite me and sitting, his large body dwarfing the small table and chairs.

"Yes, I know you're not the Jupiter from my dreams, and I'm not the Millicent you've been spying on." For years prior to my immortality, Alexandre presented himself to me while I slept. As he waited for me to mature, he comforted me in a gentle and loving way, always walking me down the same path, the path that would lead me here. In my dreamlike state, I imagined him as Jupiter, the Roman god. Alexandre did resemble the gods with his head of full blond hair, sharp features, and strong, powerful body, so why shouldn't I have thought of him in that way?

Alexandre narrowed his eyes, sweeping his gaze over my face and body. "What do you mean?"

"I mean, for me, this has already happened." I waved my hand around in the air. "I've already met you; you've turned me into a vampire, and we've lived together in America for over two hundred years." I passed a hand over my brow. "I know I sound unhinged, but it's true."

Alexandre blinked his eyes, the corners of his mouth turned down more in confusion than a frown. As I walked through the woods, I thought how best to use this Alexandre to my advantage. If I told him that I meet another man and fall in love, he would never help me. In fact, I suspect he would do everything in his power to keep me from meeting Julien in the first place. It was imperative this Alexandre believe he and I were still living happily ever after in the future.

"I'm sorry, my dear, you've completely bewildered me. Are you saying you have somehow traveled through time?"

He was always a smart man, deviously so. "That's exactly what I'm saying. Something or someone has sent me back, away from you and everything we have."

Alexandre shrugged his shoulders. "This doesn't sound like much of a problem to me. If we are as happy as you say, I don't see the harm of living it all over, again, beginning now."

I smiled sweetly, leaning forward to place my hand on his. This was exactly what I didn't want to do. "My fear is the smallest change will cause everything we have in the future to fall apart. I know this won't make sense to you now, but there are works of fiction that speculate on time travel and how any little thing can irreparably damage the future, not only for myself, but everyone. How can one remember every action one has made for two hundred years? It's impossible, and it's a terrible burden to place on me. No, I must go back, then I presume the old me, the one from this time, will re-appear. You can still experience life with her, and it will be fresh for you both."

Alexandre gripped my hand, bringing it to his lips. He closed his eyes and pressed his mouth to the back of my fingers. As he kissed me, he inhaled the scent of my skin as if he would possess every little part of me. "To have you here, in this cabin with me. I've been waiting a long time. Perhaps we can take advantage of the situation before we work on how to send you back."

You mean you can take advantage of the situation, I thought. My stomach wrenched in my gut. Not only did I have to avoid sleeping with Charles, but I also had to avoid Alexandre's bed, as well. I squeezed his hand then pulled my own from his grasp.

"Naughty Alexandre." I giggled and tried not to throw up as I batted my eyelashes. "Now is not the time. You'll have your fun with me soon enough."

Alexandre raised an eyebrow. "I've no doubt. Disappointed though I am, they do say patience is a virtue."

I affected a coquettish face, dipping my head behind my shoulder and batting my eyes some more. I wanted to slap myself, but I had to make sure Alexandre was firmly wrapped around my little finger and ready to do everything I bid.

"Your reward will be great. In the meantime, perhaps we can talk about how to get me out of my predicament."

Alexandre laughed, shaking his head and leaning back in his chair. "I've no idea. You're the one from the future, I thought you would tell me."

My hopes deflated in one sentence. I bit the inside of my cheek, my shoulders slumping forward. "No, I haven't any ideas either, which is why I'm here. Do you know of anything that could send a person through time? A demon of some sort, maybe?"

"A demon? No, demons don't exist, as far as I know." He stared at me, a blank look on his face.

I shoved the chair back, propelling myself to my feet. "Okay, you don't know anything about demons. What about…" I paced the length of the room, my arms crossed in front of my chest.

Alexandre tapped on the top of the table. "I've heard stories of witches. I know magic and mystical entities swirl around us; I believe my servant of old was a bit of a mystic."

I came to a halt. "Witches, mystics, this is a good place to start." The words were vague, but they gave me something to hold on to. "Where would we find a witch?"

Alexandre shrugged. "I couldn't say. I'm not sure they really exist."

Alexandre wasn't giving me what I needed. He wasn't as motivated as I was to find a solution. I cringed as I realized what I would have to do. I wouldn't sleep with him, but I had to give him something to get his rear end out of that chair and out into the world to find me a witch. Manipulation of this kind made me sick, but desperate times called for desperate measures. I tried to tell myself Alexandre was not yet a good person, that he will murder Julien and spend the next two centuries attempting to manipulate me, then murder Kathryn Hart, and almost Jack, Annie, and myself. Suddenly, I didn't feel so bad anymore.

Resolve flowing through me, I held my hand out. Alexandre slid his palm against mine and I tugged him into a standing position. Taking a deep breath, I moved my body against him, sliding my hands over his chest and around his neck. "My powerful Alexandre. There's nothing you can't do."

He gazed down at me with hooded eyes, his large, strong hands moving around my waist.

Angling my head, I pushed myself up on my toes. Alexandre bent forward to meet my kiss halfway, his lips eager for mine. He gripped me tighter, crushing me to him, his lips a breath away. It took every ounce of willpower I had to not pull away. I couldn't do it; this was a line I could not cross. Instead of kissing him, I veered my head to the side, pressing my face into the side of his neck. I hugged Alexandre tight, my lips grazing his throat. Jack was the reason I was doing this, and I had every intention of telling him what I did to get home to him. He may want to murder Alexandre, but this was a necessary evil.

Alexandre swooped his arm down to pick me up. He meant to take me to the bed. I stumbled back, taking his hands in mine and dropping a kiss on his knuckles. "I can't lay with you. Not while I'm so anxious over our future. Besides, I must get back to the chateau. I only hope our lives will work out as they should."

I released Alexandre's hands and took two steps back. His face was pained. "You're right. We must correct this wrong. I will set out at sunset tomorrow to find someone who can help us. Even if I must scour the globe, I'll do it for you, my love." His eyes smoldered like fire. Once again, I felt a tinge of guilt for how I played him, but I quickly pushed it away. *Keep thinking of him as the Alexandre of old.*

"I knew I could count on you. I can always count on my Jupiter." I brought my fingers to my lips to blow Alexandre a kiss before departing back into the night.

CHAPTER EIGHT

Alexandre

The air in the kitchen was thick. Tension threaded through the space like a palpable entity. The look on Jack's face was one of pure devastation. His eye twitched as he swept his gaze away from Thayer. The wrinkle on Jack's brow was so tight it looked painful. For a second, I almost felt sorry for him. I was afraid to let my own pain show. It was true, I was no longer in love with Millicent. But I felt a protectiveness over her I had never felt for anyone else except Bria. What I didn't want was for Bria to wonder.

Tash must have caught the look on Jack's face because he said, "They will both be here before we know it. If you'll give me ten minutes to prepare and set up, I can perform the spell. Selene, will you help me carry this stuff out back?"

Selene stuck the gas station maps under her arm and gathered up a pile of baggies that Tash pointed to. The bags contained herbs he would need for his spells. Tash scooped up a mortar and pestle, and an item wrapped in cloth I suspected was a dagger.

He and Selene led the way out back. The rest of us followed like obedient soldiers.

Tash chose a spot in the middle of the well-clipped lawn and dropped down to his knees. "This should do," he muttered.

He sat down his burden then reached to take Selene's. The night was a beautiful one, serene, peaceful. The sounds of the forest beyond the lawn were natural ones; spring insects, tree limbs creaking in the light breeze. The sky was not entirely clear as cloud cover had rolled in during the afternoon and hung billowy and unthreateningly over us, a few stars peeking out here and there. The smell of clover was soft and relaxing.

The warm glow from the chateau provided Tash all he needed to see. He hadn't asked for more light.

Bria stepped away from me, her eyes glued to Tash's various implements. She was intrigued. "Will you need any help, Tash?" she asked, likely hoping the answer would be yes.

Tash shook his head as he organized his items around him on the grass. "No, what I'll need is space. I know everyone will want to watch, which is fine, just please give me a good, solid perimeter. Sometimes, a spell can go wrong and hit someone it wasn't intended to."

I reached out and gently pulled Bria by her elbow. "Meaning you and the baby should stay back even further."

Bria turned back to me, sticking out her tongue. "I'm not letting you tell me what to do. I was already thinking that." She shoved into me playfully and we stepped farther away from the others.

Grace came out and plopped herself down on the terrace steps, not at all interested in what her dad was doing. She sipped juice out of a box and moved her feet like she would rather be doing anything else in the world. I glanced back at her.

"I didn't want to be alone." She shrugged.

"Okay, here we go. Everyone stay quiet, please, no matter what happens. I need to focus all my concentration on the task at hand." Tash knelt in the grass; the spells he would cast laid out in three piles around him.

The first was the locator spell. We had already seen him perform this at the lake's edge to find Mills. Once again, Tash pierced the tip of a finger with the dagger pulled from the cloth. This he dropped into his mortar along with a strand of Annie's hair and a few pinches of herbs from his baggies. He ground his ingredients and then poured out the small dollop onto the map. The air crackled with energy.

Tash nodded his head. The spell would tell him what we all already knew. He only wanted to be thorough. I thought his precise nature was promising.

Everyone held their collective breath and watched with eager eyes as the drop moved around the surface and came to rest on the area of Salem. She was not where we assumed she would be. In my mind, I saw Annie as I had then, a small but strong beauty in a plain gown, her face glowing with youth and vitality.

"Salem?" Tash looked up, making eye contact with me.

"No idea," I said.

Selene walked over and crouched down next to the map, a smile on her face. "I like this woman. She's not sitting idly by, waiting to be rescued. She's making the attempt to rescue herself."

"Of course, she is. Like I said. What's the chance she'll find a witch there?" From my vantage point, I could see a side angle of Thayer's face. His smile was broad, proud.

Tash regarded Thayer, one eyebrow raised. "Pretty good, actually. If she has found one, and that witch combines her powers with mine, we'll really be in business."

I, too, was proud of Annie. "Her location shouldn't matter, should it? We can continue?"

"We can continue with renewed hope." Tash motioned for Selene to move away.

The second spell was the binding spell. For this spell, Tash took a single thread of dark hair and wound it tightly around his wrist. As the hair spiraled his flesh, he whispered words I couldn't make out. The air sparked a little more intensely this time. Tash told us this would happen. As the magic he performed was layered, each spell would intensify as it built on the last.

There was nothing tangible for us to see other than the small flashes of light around the witch. This was the only indication we had that the spell was effective. I wondered if Annie would feel anything on her side. Would she see the sparks? Would she feel like something was happening? I hoped she wouldn't be afraid. Not my rebel.

Time for the final act, to pull Annie from the past back to where she belonged. Tash looked up, long enough to make eye contact with Selene. Selene stood the closest to him in her usual lounge wear, the least vampiric-looking immortal I'd ever seen. She smiled softly, giving Tash all the encouragement he needed to continue. I still wasn't convinced this union would be a successful one, but what did I know?

My gaze flitted to Jack and Thayer, standing so close together, I was surprised they weren't holding each other. Thayer's hands were balled into fists at his sides, his face set like stone. We all formed an odd semi-circle around Tash.

This was it. Tash returned his attention to his piles of magical objects. He again took up the mortar. Into this went more of his blood and herbs. He ground this together, then stopped and looked up at Thayer.

Tash's brow wrinkled with a thought. "When I brought back Selene, I used my own blood, obviously, but I thought it might have worked because I already felt a connection with her. Maybe…"

Thayer leaped forward, his hand outstretched. "Maybe because of my connection with Annie, my blood will be useful."

Tash nodded. "I assume vampires don't have diseases. So, I don't have to worry about disinfecting this, right?"

"You'll be fine," Selene offered.

Tash pressed the tip of his knife into Thayer's index finger, moving the mortar to catch the crimson drops.

When Tash had all he needed, he pushed away Thayer's hand. Tash placed the pestle back inside the bowl, his words becoming a loud chant in the night. It was a good thing this house was so detached from the town.

More sparks filled the air around us. It was almost beautiful. The zings of white and blue swirled by like small comets, a light show just for us. All at once, another strange phenomenon occurred. A strange wind swept over the lawn, picking up all of Tash's implements and scattering them out of his reach. This wind was oddly familiar. My stomach dropped to my toes.

"It's her," Selene said, digging in her heels against the assault.

Bria leaned her face into my shoulder, and I shielded my eyes as bits of dirt and leaves assaulted my face. I heard Tash curse and forced an eye open to see what was happening. He was reaching out for the mortar, the contents of which spilled out over the deep green of the grass.

As abruptly as the wind picked up, it died. I cleaned out the corners of my eyes the best I could. As I did so, a woman appeared, directly in front of Tash. Her back was to me and Bria as if she didn't consider either of us a threat. Thayer and Jack stood off to the newcomer's left, gaping at her like she was some sort of devil.

To her right stood Selene doing something I had never seen her do. She was baring her fangs. Selene moved her right foot behind her as if she meant to leap at this woman and tear her to shreds. It was then I realized who this strange person must be. I hadn't taken the woman's dress into consideration, my sight being compromised at first. This was Nephthys.

I reached out and pushed Bria behind my back. I thought she would fight me, but she didn't. Bria moved behind me, and I felt her body turn. She was looking to see where Grace was. If Grace remained as she was on the steps, she would be directly behind Bria, at least two bodies away from danger.

"Nephthys, please. What do I have to do to get you to stop this?" Selene was angry. I could hear it in her sharp tone of voice, but she was trying at diplomacy.

"There's nothing you can do but accept the fate of your friends. Had the witch not bound you and these other two to this realm"—Nephthys swept her hand in the direction of Thayer and Jack—"I would put you all back where you belong, before you became immortal. As it is, I will have to make do with the two I have and come for the rest of you, later. His spell will wear off eventually. Don't worry about the females, I'll make sure they never receive the tainted blood of an immortal. I told you, Selene. You cannot cheat death. Death will always win in the end."

For the first time in my life, I was at a loss for words. I would have given anything for my immortal strength back simply to rush at this creature and break her in two. Out of all of them, why did she choose Millicent and Annie? My gaze ran to the two lumps of worthless nothings to the left of the goddess. She could have taken Jack and Thayer and done us all a service, instead, this evil goddess chose to take my eternal companions.

My mind raced with possibilities. Surely there was something I could do. As my thoughts swirled, Jack, who'd been looking down for a few beats, slowly turned his head to regard the goddess. The deadly look in his eye almost forced me a step back.

With the speed and power of a freight train, he launched himself into the air and tackled Nephthys around the waist, pinning her arms at her sides. I couldn't have been more shocked. My head snapped toward Selene, who crouched down, ready to pounce next.

There was a flash of light behind my eyes. I saw something, something I didn't remember ever happening. Was this from my new past with Millicent? "Bite her, Jack. Bite her, now!" I shouted.

"Can we bind her?" Selene yelled to Tash.

Tash looked as shocked as I was by what was happening,

but quickly shook it off as he regathered his items.

Jack didn't hesitate, he clamped his mouth to the neck of the goddess and drank. He held her tight as she writhed, spittle slipping down her cheeks in her fury. Then, she was gone.

Jack stumbled forward onto his knees; his head bowed toward the ground.

Thayer ran to him, leaning over and reaching out a hand. "Are you all right? What happened?"

Jack clearly needed a minute. He shook his head from side to side, as if gathering his wits. I was impressed. I never would have thought Jack had it in him to attack anyone, and so fiercely. Yes, he had taken off my head, but he was never really in the fray of that explosive battle. I was almost proud of him.

Tash and Selene stared, while Jack took Thayer's hand and stood up on shaky feet. "Her blood was unlike anything I've ever tasted. The power was incredible, I could feel it flowing from her to me. If she hadn't disappeared, I wouldn't have stopped."

"You just drank the blood of a goddess. Your strength will increase ten-fold," I said, momentarily jealous again.

Selene looked at me, perplexed. "Why did you tell him to drink from her, Alexandre?"

I shook my head, unsure of where the idea came from. "I don't know. It was almost like déjà vu, like I'd done it before, but I don't remember when."

Jack's head snapped in my direction. "Maybe you drank from her in the past, the past where Millicent currently is."

"Maybe. The thought did occur to me. This means they're changing the timeline, but we're all still here, so I guess that's a good thing." My words flew out one after the next. "Is she gone, though? Surely, it's not that easy."

Selene shook her head. "It's not, you probably only bought us some time, but every moment is precious. She may be weakened, but she'll return." Selene looked down at Tash. "Can we continue with the spell?"

Tash sat with his hands propped on his knees. "I know you want to get to work now, but we need to do this the right way. I must be at full strength, and we will have to start over. I'm going to need a few hours to recharge. Every time I perform a spell, no matter how small, it takes a toll."

Bria sighed, still behind me, her head resting on my back. "Let's hope Nephthys stays away that long."

CHAPTER NINE

Annie

Was I really this lucky? The first witch I happened upon in Salem was Tash's ancestor. I wanted to jump for joy. Abigail sat opposite, her face one of uncertainty with one eyebrow sharply raised as she regarded me.

It was time to press my case. I leaned forward, hands clasped in front of me on the table. "It seems that by helping me, you help your descendant. How fortuitous for us both."

The witch nodded slowly, her pale, red hair falling around her face. "Tell me about him."

My stomach knotted as I thought through what to say. I didn't know Tash, at all. Not really. We met and were in each other's presence for a grand total of ten minutes. She was able to deduce my name. Would she know if I lied to her? I decided the best course of action was to tell the truth. The most important thing was keeping this woman on my side.

"To be honest, I don't know him well. His name is Tash and he helped an acquaintance return one of the four horsemen of the apocalypse to Hell. He and this woman became quite close, which is why he's helping us now. Tash also has a daughter named Grace, who is sweet and lovely. That's all I can tell you as Tash was only recently introduced to me through the acquaintance, my maker's sister."

"Your maker?" interrupted Abigail. "You're not a vampire."

I sighed, shaking my head. "No, I'm not yet. But I was in the past, and I will be in the future." I dropped my face into my hands. "It's hard to explain."

"Good thing I have all day. I'll make us some tea. When was the last time you ate?"

My stomach felt as hollow as an empty tube. "I ate a muffin a few minutes ago, but before that—two hundred and fifty years."

Abigail snorted as she got up from her seat. "So, you're hungry then. I have some biscuits and blackberry jam."

My mouth started to water on cue. "Let me help." I moved to join her.

Abigail beckoned with a hand as she walked through the small opening to the kitchen. Her demeanor seemed to change once I mentioned her descendant. I was hopeful she would continue to be accommodating. "This way. The kettle's full. All you need to do is light the stove."

While I waited for the water to boil, I pulled two chipped but clean porcelain cups from a shelf and placed them on the table. Abigail handed me a cracked bowl of sugar and a small pitcher of milk. These were also placed on the table.

Abigail brought out a crock of jam from the larder and pulled a basket of fresh biscuits from the butcher block counter. When the tea was brewed and poured out into the cups, we sat down to our morning repast.

I wanted to be dainty and polite, but the hole in my stomach screamed to be filled. I took two biscuits, slathered them both with the dark, gooey jam and shoved the top half of the first into my mouth. My eyes closed as I savored the dreamy sweetness of the jam and the crumbly texture of the biscuit in my mouth.

Abigail snorted again. "I guess it has been a while. Don't

give yourself a belly ache, girl." She blew over the top of her steaming cup to cool it before taking a sip. She set the cup back on the table and fixed me in her intense stare. "Just because I have all day doesn't mean I want you to take all day. Feel free to tell your story at any time."

I chuckled into my cup, gulping down a too big mouthful of scalding liquid. "Ah," I sputtered as my throat burned. "I see why you blew on it, now." I was a child relearning the basics.

Abigail watched me without speaking. What I wanted to do was continue devouring the airy pillows of bread, but she was ready for me to go on.

"All right. I'm not sure where to begin. At the beginning, I guess." I paused, taking a deep breath so I could get this all out as quickly as possible. "In a very short time, a few weeks, I believe, I will meet two vampires who will grant me immortality. Other things will happen, but I want to stick to what's important for us. Fast forward two hundred and fifty years later. My best friend, and one of the two vamps I meet very soon, disappears from her house in France. We enlist assistance to find her. One of those people is a witch, Tash Allerton. Like I said, he's the boyfriend of my maker's sister, Selene, and he met her in Romania fighting demons. I know this is weird and confusing."

Abigail munched a biscuit, her face unbothered. "I'm following."

"Okay. Well, right after Tash arrives, he performs a locator spell, so we can find my friend, Millicent. He finds her in Burgundy, the region of France where she's from. Only she's there and she isn't. It comes out that Selene has called forth an Egyptian goddess of death for her guidance with another problem. The goddess was not happy and long story short, she has pulled Millicent and me back in time. I've no idea if she shot anyone else through time, so I'm working on the assumption that it's just me and Mills."

"Interesting. This is certainly not the boring morning I expected when I rose from bed." Abigail continued to eat.

"Is your maker's sister a vampire, too? Selene?"

I nodded a yes as I chewed on another mouthful.

"But Tash hasn't been…turned?" There was a strange inflection to her voice.

I shook my head. "No."

Abigail took a breath, her gaze intense. "Good. Help ensure he stays the way he is, and I'll help you. If he takes the blood, he won't last long. His coven will come for him and come for him quick."

"Okay. I'll make sure of it. I take it there's a reason why he shouldn't become one of us?" I wiped a crumb from my lip, suddenly uncomfortable.

"The power of a witch who becomes a vampire increases exponentially. No one knows exactly how much, because they have always been hunted down within the first days of immortality. It's thought that this power changes the witch, turns them evil. Protect my descendant, Annie, please." Her eyes went from hard to pleading.

"I will, I promise." I paused, looking around the room once more. "Do you have a coven?" If Abigail belonged to a coven, they didn't live here.

"I do. We are still forced to hide ourselves. There are three women in Salem, and a man and woman not far in Concord. There are six of us."

"You'll be happy to know it won't always be like this. There will come a time when you won't have to fear imprisonment." I smiled at Abigail, but she didn't smile back.

If my strange tale of vampires and demons had shocked her, she didn't seem perturbed in the least. Part of me wondered if she fully believed me. Maybe she thought I was mad. I was beginning to feel like I could be.

She popped the last bit of food in her mouth and washed it down with some tea. "When in time is your friend?"

"That's another crazy thing. She and I were contemporaries, so she must be in France right now as we speak." I could no longer hold myself back from eating.

While I chewed, Abigail sipped at her tea as if we were having the most normal of conversations.

She looked thoughtful, her brows pushed slightly together, her gaze trained on the tabletop. I allowed her time to think as I finished off my plate. When I was full and I could no longer bear the silence, I spoke. "Do you believe me?"

Her gaze met mine, her eyes crinkling at the corners in a soft smile. "Oh, I believe you. There was something about your energy when you strolled about my storefront. I noticed it right away. Magic is just the manipulation of energy and your energy has been manipulated in a way I've never seen before. You've been on a long journey, Annie. I suspect you will travel even farther by the time this is over."

"I have to ask, again. How did you know my name?"

"My familiar told me."

"Your what?" I scrunched up my face, looking around the small room. There was nothing here but the two of us.

Abigail craned her neck back and spoke to the quiet. "Come out, Grimal."

My attention flicked to the dark far corner of the room where I sensed movement. As I stared, two golden eyes began to glow. With deliberate slowness, a lanky, coal-black cat sauntered its way from the shadow. Grimal walked with his head down and his eyes up, trained on me as if I were his prey. I didn't know whether to like him or fear him.

The sleek animal came to a stop alongside his mistress, plopping onto his rear, his eyes never leaving me. Abigail reached down and scratched the top of his head. The cat purred as any normal feline would.

"Right, so your cat knew my name. But, how? He's a cat." My gaze moved from Grimal to Abigail and back again. I began to squirm under the scrutiny of the feline.

"He's not a cat, not entirely. He's a familiar. A familiar is a magical creature, almost in every way as powerful as a witch. Like attracts like. We move through life with one another, always watching the other's back. Grimal is especially adept at learning names. You would be surprised how important it can be to know the true name of someone who would deceive you."

I tried to relax back in my chair, my neck starting to feel tense from all the anxiety. "I get it. I didn't know there were such things as demons in the world until recently, and I suppose they must hide their true form all the time." I wondered why familiars were not similarly attracted to vampires. Watching Grimal sit obediently next to his mistress caused me a little jealousy. How wonderful it would be to have my own familiar, a companion and a partner. I would have to think on this more, later.

"Indeed." Abigail continued to stroke Grimal's head.

I shifted my attention back to Abigail. "You said you believe me, but you never said for sure that you would help me."

Abigail inclined her head. "I said I'll help you if you keep Tash from the blood, soon-to-be-vampire. It's good for you that you're not immortal yet. I can't stand immortals, tricky beasts." Abigail looked down, her face twisted in thought. "I knew a vampire once. He was so beautiful, but his face was a lie."

My attention perked up and I scooted closer in my chair. "What happened to him?"

"I was a young woman, just past my twentieth year. He tried to seduce me, lure me. I knew what he wanted. To deny him took all my self-possession, but had I given in, he would have turned me into an abomination. I worked a spell on him. Someone had to teach him a lesson."

Abigail had my full attention. "What was the spell? Did you turn him into a frog?"

She laughed, pulling her hand away from Grimal to cover her mouth. "I should have. No, I made him stink like dying weeds. He stayed far away from me after that."

I smiled, loving the idea of a vampire out in the world who smelled of rotting vegetation. "I like it."

"Yes, the spell was a good one. What is the name of this

Egyptian goddess who sent you here?"

"Nephthys, I think. There was so much going on at the time, but I'm pretty sure that's the name I heard."

Abigail shrugged her shoulders. "Never heard of her, but that doesn't matter. I would like a little something in return for my work. I'm sure you understand this."

Of course, I thought. I pursed my lips, the tension in my neck increasing ten-fold. "On top of guarding your descendant. What is it you'd like?"

Her gaze slid over my face. "Only a lock of your hair. Surely, a little hair isn't much to ask for."

Instinctively, my hand flew up to my head. "Why on earth do you want my hair?"

Abigail shook her head with another snort. "According to you, you've been immortal, and will be again. A small bit of hair can hold a lot, it's an extension of a soon to be powerful being. I could use it in all manner of spells."

I relaxed, moving my hand down to my lap. "And that's all? You aren't taking a piece of my soul with my hair?"

"Not to worry. My powers and my family name are all I have. Four of my ancestors were accused of witchcraft less than a hundred years ago, here in this very town. Two perished by the hands of the townspeople, one at the gallows and one in a cell. The others escaped their captors, leaving to live elsewhere while the hysteria continued. They were rescued and sheltered by others like them. Witches take care of our own. Most of the people who did actually die during those horrible times were human, completely innocent of witchcraft."

"Why do you remain here after what happened?"

"Salem is my home. Not only that, but it's an old town with an ancient power. The power that comes from the ground is useful. Humans will do what they will do. If we remain in the shadows, that history should be over. Sad, isn't it?"

"It is." My initial fears over Abigail left me. She wasn't a frightening woman. Eccentric maybe, but not frightening.

"What do we do now?" I leaned forward, ready to get on with the ceremonies. It took everything in my power to ignore the pain and exhaustion in my human body. A body I was eager to leave behind.

"Now, we call upon the dark star."

CHAPTER TEN

Alexandre

Shaken did not begin to describe my demeanor. It took all my inner power to appear as if I was keeping a level head. I wasn't. Nephthys shocked me. We didn't know enough about her or what she could do to have a firm understanding of what we were up against.

It seemed Jack had sent her away for the time being by attacking and drinking from her, but if I knew anything about otherworldly beings, and I knew a little, this was not the end.

Our motley crew had reassembled back in the kitchen, taking up our usual spots. Tash was going to wave his magic wand and make a second attempt at retrieving Annie. I was relieved, glad she would soon be safely returned to us. Worry bloomed through me for both of my children, but for Millicent, it bloomed the fullest. The longer they were out there, the more danger they were in.

I wondered if Mills would seek me out, look for me at the little stone cabin. What would I do? How would I respond? There wasn't much doubt that the me of old would act in whatever way was the most selfish. She needed to be rescued or Millicent would find herself at my mercy. Guilt prickled its way along my spine, winding itself around my belly until I was sick with it. We had to work fast, before Nephthys could strike again.

Bria moved up next to me, the scent of her citrus hair washing over me like calm waters. "Alexandre, what is it?" She wrapped her small, strong hand around my elbow.

"He's going to hurt her, I know it." I spoke in a low tone, not wanting the others to hear me.

"Who's going to hurt who?" Bria asked in a shaky whisper. "Nephthys is a woman."

"I'm going to hurt Mills, not Nephthys." My voice was quiet, but not quiet enough in a room full of immortals. Jack's gaze slid toward me, murderous hatred hot behind his sharp blue eyes. He was keyed up after drinking the goddess's blood. There was no doubt in my mind he could take me out with a flick of his fingers. Fear of what the others would think of him was likely the reason he held back.

Bria pulled me closer. "None of us can know what's happening. They could both be asleep in their beds for all we know."

"Annie's not," said Thayer, leaning against his favorite wall like a stone. "She's trying to get herself back. You saw the map, the same as all of us. She's in Salem looking for recruits."

Bria snapped her head sharply in his direction. "I'm trying to soothe him."

I nodded at Thayer. "And that puts her in further danger. Mills, too, is different now. She'll try something, anything she can think of."

Bria pushed herself up, pressing a feathery kiss against my cheek. She turned toward Tash at the kitchen island. "Okay, things have changed. We need to get them both back, now. You can't bring them both through at the same time because it will expend too much energy. What if you siphon energy from us? Is that possible?"

If it was possible to love her more, I did at that moment. Bria's question was simple yet brilliant. If there was one thing I had learned over the last few weeks, it was that nothing was truly impossible.

Tash leaned over his hands, gripping the sides of the island. He rocked back and forth for a moment, gazing down at the objects sitting around his black box. "Maybe," he muttered and fell silent again.

No one else in the room spoke as we all stared at a man none of us really knew. I realized this witch was our salvation. We were relying on a near-stranger for a lot.

Tash shifted on his feet, still gazing down, and he said, "I'll already be drawing on the power of the dark star to pull them through time. To draw on anything else will be tricky."

"What's the dark star?" Selene had moved from the small pedestal kitchen table and now stood behind Tash, leaning against the lip of the farmhouse sink.

"The dark star is a magical object. It's a huge chunk of black opal. The gemstone was imbued by magic so long ago that no one really knows its origins. It's housed in a vault somewhere in England near Bakewell. The power of the stone has been used for centuries, at least, by every witch who knows about it."

"You don't have to be near it to use its energy?" The curious look on Selene's face was one I'd seen many times since meeting her. She was deeply fascinated by all things mystical.

"No. A witch can be anywhere in the world and draw from the dark star. All one needs to know is the proper spell." Tash stepped back, facing the group and bringing Selene into the circle. "I already used it once, to pull you back. So, I know I can use it again, along with my other spells. But, siphoning energy from you"—Tash waved his hand around—"that will be hard. I'm not sure I can handle it. Therefore, I need another witch."

"What about me, Daddy?" Grace peered at her father from the table.

Tash didn't speak as he seemed to be considering her words. "I don't know, Grace."

I wanted to encourage them both but didn't feel it was my place to involve myself with Tash's child. If he used her for the spell, the decision would have to be his alone. By speaking up, Grace had answered a question I'd had since meeting her. Was she a witch, too?

"I'll be fine, Dad. It's a simple siphoning spell. I won't be directly involved, just off to the side, sucking energy from the vamps. They have plenty to spare, and even if I take a little too much, it won't kill them. Then, I'll direct it at you. I'll be like a conduit, or something."

Bria snorted a laugh. Tash looked around, a proud smile on his face. "It looks like I have help, after all."

Jack sank back against the table, visibly calmer than he'd been since we gathered. Thayer reached out a hand, clasping his friend on the shoulder. Their eyes met and Jack attempted a wan half-smile.

Relief flooded through me as I thought of Annie and Millicent. If they could hold on a little longer, we would soon have them back. They could continue their lives with the bores they'd chosen, and I could get on with mine.

Tash scooped up a couple of loose herbs, placing them back into his worn, metal box. "We'll need a wide-open space. For the energy we need to generate, it'll be best if there are no other people, buildings, or even trees around. Nothing that can catch fire. Anyone know of a place like that?"

"Actually, yes. What about the location of Millicent's old home? There's nothing there now but fields. The tree line is quite far back from the center of the estate. Plus, the old chateau may be gone, but the gravel drive is still there. It's circular and large." I knew all this because I was recently there, licking my wounds after the showdown with Mills, Annie, and Jack in Savannah. The cabin seemed like a good refuge at the time, and it still stood after all these years.

I purposely avoided Jack's eyes as I related the second

part. "And the cabin where I waited for Mills remains. It's protected, should the immortals need to retreat there during daylight hours."

Tash's face was full of questions. He had no idea what I was talking about, but he shrugged his shoulders anyway. "Sounds ideal. How long will it take to get there? If we can be there in less than an hour, I say we do this tonight. Why waste any more time? And we can be rest assured that Nephthys will soon be back."

Everyone looked to me as I realized I was the most familiar with that area. "Annie was back and forth in a matter of minutes. If we all hitch rides with the immortals, I'd say it would take us five minutes."

Grace stood up from the table, her small hands placed on top. "Bria should stay behind. No offense. I've heard from Selene that you're super-cool, but I'm not taking energy that you need for your baby."

Tash nodded, his head turning toward Bria. "Grace is right. I'm sure you want to help, but it will be better for everyone if you stay behind."

Bria smiled warmly at Grace. "I wasn't planning on going but thank you for being concerned. I'll be tucking myself into bed. I'm only staying up to see you all off."

"What about me? Will you be able to use any of my energy?" I wasn't sure if my weakened state as a mortal would be helpful, but I was going whether they needed me or not.

Tash said, "Probably not. You can help me organize everything I'll need." Tash turned his head toward Selene. "And we should have a plan for how to deal with Nephthys. If she shows up again, she'll throw everything off."

Selene's brow wrinkled. "If only we could bind her like you did War."

Tash shook his head. "No way I can deviate from the other spells. We need another idea."

"Do you think you can siphon enough energy from Jack and Thayer? If so, I can hide in wait with a sword, attacking her if she materializes. Maybe if I'm fast enough, she won't have the time to react." Selene's idea was a solid one. If anyone could chop a goddess to bits, it was my sister.

Jack stepped forward. "Sounds like a good plan to me. Make sure you aim for her head."

Tash shrugged. "It's the best we've got. If I feel like the spell needs more juice, we'll have no option but to use you, Selene. But until then, you'll stay off to the side."

"Okay." Selene moved forward, ready to take charge. "I'll carry my brother. Thayer will take Tash and Jack will take Grace and the bundle of items our witches will need. Tash, what can we do to get out the door in a timely fashion?"

Selene was thoughtful, offering to take me to the old chateau. I couldn't even begin to imagine the awkwardness of riding with Thayer and especially not with Jack. I imagined an accident taking place along the way where I lose my head, this time without the possibility of it reattaching. I reminded myself to thank her, later.

"Everything I need is in this box, even my herbs." He continued to gather his magical items, picking objects up with care and placing them back into the various compartments of the battered container. He had a brass bell, a tiny hand broom, his knife wrapped in cloth, plastic baggies of dried and fresh herbs, the mortar and pestle, and a bunch of other little things I was unable to identify.

Once the box was packed and secured, Tash slipped it inside a backpack and handed it to Jack. "Don't lose this. And especially, don't lose that." Tash pointed to Grace, who giggled, running to her dad who scooped her up in a fierce hug.

I glanced down at Bria's still flat stomach. It was hard to imagine that in a few months we would have a child of our own. Something about it hadn't seemed real to me. It still didn't. I supposed once the baby came, he or she would feel real in a flash. I wondered if my child would look at me with eyes full of love the way Grace looked at Tash.

"I'll walk you guys out." Bria took my hand, pulling me along after her, out of the kitchen and down the hallway. "I know what you're thinking, Alexandre," she said over her shoulder.

"You can't possibly know what I'm thinking," I grumbled.

"Pretty sure I do. You're going to be a great dad. Don't worry about it." Bria squeezed my hand as we stopped in front of the door.

"Me, worried? No way." I leaned down, slipping an arm around her waist and lifting her up. "Lock this door tight after we leave." I crushed her to me, capturing her perfect mouth with mine.

I released her and opened the door. She reached out to brush my back with her fingertips. "Be careful, Alexandre. Don't do anything stupid."

Right at that moment, Jack was passing behind me and out the door. I distinctly heard him snicker.

Once we were all assembled outside and Bria was locked in the house, we arranged ourselves. Jack secured the backpack and then cradled Grace in his arms. She was tall for her age, and her long legs dipped down, causing him a little difficulty. I smiled.

Selene crouched down so I could hop on her back. Even though I had her by about four inches, she held onto me with ease. The only one left was Tash. He looked at the rest of us, then back to Thayer, who stood with his back to Tash, ready for him to hop on.

"I'm supposed to ride piggyback, how far?" Tash looked back at Selene, who laughed out loud.

"Yes, you are. I know it's strange, but it's only for a few minutes. You'll be fine. This in no way diminishes your masculinity. Promise."

With that, laughter broke out everywhere. Tash wrinkled his brow. "That's not why...it's just weird...oh, never mind," he stammered, eliciting snorts and chuckles all around.

Tash placed his hands on Thayer's shoulders and jumped up.

Thayer spoke to the road ahead. "Hold on, here we go."

We were there in no time. As awkward as I felt on Selene's back, I knew Tash felt worse. The immortals were all relieved of their burdens and we went to work. The center of the graveled drive was a perfect, level space, as I'd thought. There were few weeds to contend with, even after all this time.

Tash sat on his knees and laid out his implements, grouping them by spell. The first spell would be to fix the exact location of the women. Second, would be the binding spell, securing their energies to Tash's. And third, would be the spell that would bring them home. The items for the locator spell were laid to his left, the binding spell to his right, and the final spell, straight ahead.

I wasn't any help at all, so I sat off to the side on a large rock to observe.

Tash held up his hands, pressing each finger as if he were making sure he had remembered everything. "Grace, I'm ready. Get them in place."

Selene swung her katana from the front of her body to her back. She disappeared into the trees. The distance was far, but she would be able to run out in a flash should Nephthys appear.

Grace took both Thayer's and Jack's hands and led them to a space not far from her dad. "Sit here, please," she said, her little girl's voice sweet and small.

The vampires plopped down on the gravel, rocks crunching beneath their weight. Grace took a seat between them and her father, crossing her legs and closing her eyes. I wondered if she would cut herself as Tash did to perform his spells, but there were no implements around her. Maybe it really was a simple spell or maybe little Grace was a better witch than her dad.

Without opening her eyes, she said, "Ready."

CHAPTER ELEVEN

Millicent

The path was darker, very much like my spirits. I wanted to sink to my knees and retch over the pine needles. Holding Alexandre as I did seemed like a strong strategic move to make at that moment. Now, I simply felt sick to my core. It was wrong to make him think I wanted him, and Jack would be furious and hurt. The more I thought about it, I was sure he wouldn't understand my thinking. He already hated Alexandre, and this was going to be the last straw. Jack would never be able to be in the same room with Alexandre again. I hadn't meant for it to, but the nuzzle felt like a betrayal.

Instead of focusing on where I was stepping, my head was down as thoughts of Jack assailed me. I needed him now. As much as I wanted to believe I was strong on my own, and I was, I was stronger with him. We made each other better. A longing greater than anything I'd ever experienced swept through me. It was because of this that I tripped over a vine and came down hard on one knee.

"Son of a…" I twisted around in the dirt, tugging at the hem of my dress snagged on a broken branch.

Movement caused me to flinch back. I peered into the dark, but without my preternatural sight, all I could see were inky, tunnel-like waves, my eyes unable to fully focus. "Who's there? Alexandre, are you following me?" My stomach dropped as I realized I shouldn't have said the name aloud. What if it was Charles who lurked in the dark? I could say I didn't care all I liked, but I still had to remain as normal as possible while I was here.

"Your vampire lover is tucked away in his cabin. You are quite alone in this enchanted forest, my pretty one." The voice was liquid silk. Her words reminded me of a fairytale witch, but her voice was that of a queen.

As I stared at the center of the path, a figure emerged. I wasn't sure if I should be frightened or not. An olive-skinned woman with long plaited hair stood in front of me looking like a hieroglyphic. Her dress was gold and barely covered her skin. Strips of a dark cloth encircled her ankles and wrists, and something large and strange sat atop her head.

I yanked my dress free, tearing the fabric, and carefully rose to my feet, never taking my eyes off the woman in front of me. "Do we know each other?" The question was tentatively asked, my voice a soft quiver in the night.

"I know you, although I doubt you've heard of me. I'm acquainted with your lover's sister, Selene. My name is Nephthys." The woman stood as still as stone, arms down at her sides like a statue.

"Alexandre is not my lover. He's my…friend." I tried to maintain a casual attitude, but intuition was screaming this woman was danger. Alexandre's sister was named Selene. I knew of her existence, but nothing more. It was revealed that Alexandre was Caesarion, the son of Julius Caesar and Cleopatra. I hadn't thought much about it, but that would make Selene the daughter of Antony and Cleopatra. Now the Egyptian dress made sense. What this woman had to do with me I couldn't fathom.

Nephthys laughed a light, sweet giggle. "It doesn't really

matter what you call him. You'll have all the time in the world to become closer, now that you're here. Although, I won't allow him to change you. No one cheats death, Millicent. The others may have thwarted me for the moment, but it's only temporary."

"Why? I don't understand why you've chosen me to torture."

"You're not special, child. I plan on pulling you all back to where you belong, then making it impossible for you to become immortal again. Since Alexandre is mortal in the future, I had planned on leaving him alone. However, now I see I must get him out of the way, so he can't help you. Sad, really, he is the son of Isis." Nephthys laughed hysterically, moving her body for the first time as she shook with devious joy.

The son of Isis? I tried to hide my shock. There were too many things going on here and I didn't know how to process it, but what I didn't want was to give this woman the satisfaction of seeing me squirm. At least one mystery had been solved; I knew why I was here. I needed to learn all I could, and as much as I hated the thought of returning to him so soon, I had to warn Alexandre.

"What does that make you then? You told me your name, but who are you to Selene and Alexandre?"

"I think I've told you all I care to. It's time to make sure your husband knows you've been sneaking about. Tell me, dear, are there locks on your bedroom door? If not, there's about to be."

The blood in my veins turned to ice. What did she intend to do, appear to Charles as an Egyptian goddess?

In answer to my question, she began to change before my eyes. The darkness filled with an eerie glow as the Egyptian woman before me turned into someone very dear. The gold dress fell away, replaced by a fine sackback gown of gold and black silk. The headdress disappeared and the long dark hair lightened and twirled itself above her head in the fashionable pouf of the day.

"Not Clea," I breathed, unable to contain the fear growing within me, my limbs beginning to shake.

"If you come with me, like a good girl, I promise to ask for leniency." Nephthys, now in the form of my old friend, held her hand out to me. What choice did I have but to follow? I couldn't turn and run back to Alexandre. This creature possessed powers greater than his. He was already in enough danger.

Just as I resolved to hold up my head and take her dreaded hand, a flash of yellow streaked out of the forest. Alexandre snatched the woman up, clamping his mouth on her throat. Nephthys gasped, flailing against the mighty body that held her close.

Alexandre must have drunk fast; she was unable to fight him off. Her body ceased to fight as her eyelids fell. Then, in a flash, she was gone, nothing but air.

"You killed her," I squealed. Unable to contain my relief, I clapped my hands together. I looked down at my body. Now that she was dead, surely her magic would disappear as well. But nothing happened.

"I don't think so. I watched from afar. If she was really Nephthys, she's a goddess, Millicent. A goddess of death. I don't have the power to kill such a superior being."

"She disappeared. Maybe you did kill her." Even as I said the words, I knew they must be untrue. I was still here, and nothing had changed.

"All I did was buy us time. She'll be back. The only question is when. In the meantime, we both need to keep an eye out for her. I hate to leave you alone, but I think I know where I need to go for help now."

My shoulders slumped under the weight of the new anxiety now surging through me like electricity. "I'll be fine, Alexandre. The only real danger I'm in is being locked up by my husband. Do what you need to."

Alexandre looked at me, his gaze on my mouth. That was not happening, no matter what. I patted his arm as I stepped around him. "I have to get back and quickly. Visit me in my dreams when you've returned and let me know what you've found."

I picked up my skirts, gaze on the dark path as I left Alexandre behind me.

There wasn't much time to think on my predicament. When I emerged from the tree line into the clearing, the rooms on the ground floor of the chateau were aglow with light. Several carriages dotted the drive with another pulling around as I walked across the lawn. There was no more hiding the fact that I was here. I would have to say I needed to take some night air. We must have been hosting a party for the evening. I tried to remember back but couldn't grab on to any firm memories of this night.

A white coiffured head poked out of the moving rose-colored carriage and my heart threatened to stop. "Millicent, my love, whatever are you doing out here?" Clea, a duchess and one of my only genuine friends from this time, stuck her silk-clad arm out the window and waved me over.

Was this my Clea or that horrible goddess? I froze halfway between the chateau and the forest, whipping my head around to look for an escape. There was none. I was woefully exposed. Balling my fists into the side of my dress, I pressed on. *Please, don't be her.*

As I reached the front of the drive, Clea was grasping the hand of one of our footmen and descending onto the gravel with dainty mint-green slippers. I stood back, observing and waiting for the woman to reveal herself.

Clea bounded toward me, her heavy silk gown, the same mint green as her slippers, bouncing along with her every stride. I wanted this to be my Clea with everything my heart could feel. "Have you not dressed for the evening? What fun, allow me to play lady's maid." My dear friend scooped me into her arms, her talcum scent almost making me cry.

"Oh, Clea, it is you." I tightened my arms around her, my face pressed to her powdery neck.

Clea held me for a beat then gently pushed me back to look in my face. "What is it? Your worthless husband?" she whispered.

"No…yes. I don't know. It's been a rough day."

Clea nodded, her warm eyes wise and knowing. "Let's get you in your finery, Marchioness. A little wine and dancing always helps."

We hooked our arms around each other and went inside. Her husband, the Duke, inclined his head as we passed.

Clea was shocked to see me without a corset. "I would never be so bold," she said as she pulled the contraption I'd always detested around me.

My friend was true to her word, dismissing Liza to help me dress herself. I suspected it was so we could talk in private. I braced myself on a bedpost, preparing to be laced.

"I'm truly sorry you have such a hard time with that cold fish you're married to, love. He has always seemed a hard man to me."

I sucked in a sharp breath as Clea cinched me without mercy. "Don't be sorry, Clea. Everything will work out as it's meant to." Even though all seemed more dire than it had before I met the goddess, I still believed I would make my way home. I had to.

"Of course, dear. If only you could get away from him for a spell. I dare say you would have a marvelous time." Clea moved to the wardrobe to pull out the yellow and white striped silk gown she had chosen for me. "This will be lovely with your golden hair."

I smiled at Clea. She had no idea that in a few weeks' time, she would have a small, impromptu gathering at her estate where I would have a very marvelous time, indeed.

After Clea had me dressed, she sat me down to do my hair. I was always a mess when it came to my own hair, but Clea was a master. She wasn't always the grand noblewoman she was now. There was a time when she'd had to do everything for herself.

While she smoothed and twisted my blonde strands, I applied some powder to my face and rouge to my cheeks.

When the duchess had my hair pinned in the exact way she desired, she secured two diamond fan-shaped pins to the back.

Citrine and diamonds dripped from my neck and my ears. The finest silk and lace clung to my body. I sat back to regard my reflection in the mirror. I realized in horror that I was reenacting a nightmare I thought long over. Never did I love this. Yes, I enjoyed my couture clothes and sparkling jewels, but the extreme opulence of my surroundings was stifling, oppressive. How I needed to get out of here.

For tonight, I would focus on the joy of being reunited with the true Clea. Then, it was back to work.

"All finished. Stand up so I can look at you." Clea patted my shoulder.

I swept up off the vanity bench and twirled around.

Clea clasped her hands. "A true beauty," she remarked, unclasping her hands and holding them out to me. "Now, let's go have some fun. This chateau needn't be gloomy all the time. First thing is the wine. We'll fill our glasses and drink 'til we're silly. Then, some dancing."

I laughed, bowing before the duchess. "As you command."

Clea giggled, scooping up my hand and walking with me out into the hall. "Viscount Richmond and his wife are here, those two are horrible bores. They'll be good company for Charles. For us, Count and Countess Dubois and the Viscount Leclerq. I will make it my mission to keep you smiling all night."

CHAPTER TWELVE

Annie

The little room was beginning to feel stifling; the pungent herbs from the space beyond mixed with odors of dampness I assumed to be from the old boards of the home. Eating had done me a world of good, but now I needed fresh air as I began to feel sweat, once again, beading around my hairline. Sadly, there appeared to be more to talk about.

"What's the dark star?" I asked Abigail.

She remained opposite me, along with her familiar who sat by her chair. Together they looked like some sort of strange painting. Abigail blinked, moving her hair back from her shoulder and breaking the spell. "The dark star is a magical object. It's far away, but that doesn't matter, we can still draw on its power to give us the energy we need to send you home."

Hope bloomed in my chest as the tension knotting every single muscle from my lower back to my neck relaxed. This sounded promising.

"Thank you, Abigail. Really, I can't thank you enough for helping me." I beamed a smile at the lady and even gazed with kindness down at Grimal.

"Don't thank me, yet. I've never sent anyone through time. I guess that doesn't mean it's impossible, though." Abigail stood, gathering up plates and teacups.

The hope, which a moment ago seemed so full, deflated a little at her words. Abigail didn't seem too confident. I closed my eyes and took a deep breath. It was important I remind myself that the others were also doing what they could. I hadn't seen Nephthys appear, so maybe with Tash working in the future and Abigail working now, their energies would somehow combine. This was new to me, too.

Wood scraped wood as I pushed back my chair to help Abigail clean up. I carried the teapot into the kitchen and set it on the well-used butcher block top.

Curious to know how soon we would begin, I asked, "What do we do first?"

Abigail had her back to me, putting away the leftovers from our morning repast in the larder. "We have a few things to do before we can make the first attempt. My morning plans involve a trip to the cemetery, then we can gather some fresh herbs."

These didn't sound like things that would get me closer to Thayer and home. I hadn't really thought of Thayer much, and now I knew why. As his form took shape in my mind, pain exploded in my heart. We had gone through so much to be together; Thayer had gone through so much. I couldn't bear the thought of him spending another two hundred and fifty years inside that coffin; Emilia's punishment for loving me and betraying her.

When Thayer thwarted Emilia Romanov's plans to decisively win the American Revolution for the English by absconding with the Culper Code Book he originally stole from me, she made sure he would never forget how he'd betrayed her. I couldn't let him go through that all over again. The past was only meant to be lived once.

Abigail must have noticed the look on my face. When she moved back into the kitchen, she placed a gentle hand on mine as it rested on the counter. "Never fear, child. We'll get you home. A good spell requires thought and preparation. It would be so much worse if we performed the spell unprepared and sent you somewhere else you didn't belong."

She had a point there. The only place I belonged was at Thayer's side. I would do anything to get back to him.

She padded out of the room, her bare feet slapping the hard ground. "Grimal will keep you company while I dress."

At his name, Grimal jumped onto the countertop, startling me so badly, I jumped back. His golden eyes regarded me with little interest, his sleek coat shiny in the light streaming through the window. The cat sat on his hind legs, his long, thin tail curling around him like a living thing that never stopped moving.

I peered into his gold eyes. This was more than a cat—I could see it in the way he watched me, his gaze narrowed just enough to show that he wasn't quite what he appeared but detached enough to look like any other feline.

"You really aren't what you seem, are you?" I whispered, more to myself than to him. I wouldn't have been surprised had he opened his mouth to speak English, but he didn't. Grimal continued to watch me, his liquid gold eyes blinking. I could have sworn the corners of his mouth twitched upward in a momentary grin, but the movement was so fast, I was sure I'd imagined it. I wasn't sure if I liked Grimal.

I pressed myself back against the sink, arms crossed in front of my chest. The cat wasn't going to move until his mistress returned, that much was clear. I squirmed under the scrutiny, attempting to look anywhere but at him.

After what felt like an eternity, Abigail returned, looking the part of an old pilgrim. She wore a simple black dress with a white collar and a white cotton cap slapped at a haphazard angle on her pale red head. She had twisted her hair into a loose bun, several strands not making it and spilling out around her face. Her feet were still bare.

I assumed she would slip on shoes at the backdoor, but she did not. Instead, she opened the door, holding it for Grimal to slink out behind her. "Coming, dear?"

I tried not to look down at Abigail's feet as we walked out and into a back alley. To my relief, Abigail pulled a pair of black boots from outside the door as she closed it. "Don't like shoes in my house," she explained as she stooped over to slip them on. She picked up a large basket next to the shoes and slung it over her arm.

I glanced down at my own feet. "I could have taken mine off."

Abigail waved her hand by way of answer. "This way." Abigail didn't wait for me, taking off down the alley and away from the town. I had to jog to catch up to her. The woman, whatever her age, was fast.

"Where are we going first?" I huffed a little, ashamed at myself for sounding so out of breath already.

"The cemetery. Before any major spell, I give thanks to my ancestors." Abigail walked with long, sure strides. It took everything I had to keep up with her on shorter legs, but I refused to fall behind.

I wasn't sure what she meant by thanks. In my mind, I imagined Abigail sacrificing a small animal over the mound of an Allerton and shuddered. "What sort of thanks?" I asked.

Abigail cackled, her voice loud in the still early morning. "The regular kind, girl. That's all."

I relaxed a little but still had no idea what she meant to do. If whatever she did got me home, I was game for almost anything.

The back streets of the town soon gave way to the forest. The scent of the pine trees was welcome, and I thought back on that long-ago night Captain Thayer Emmerich drug me through the woods of New York, toward safety and freedom. The surroundings were similar, the only difference being, this time, I could see everything by the light of the sun.

The rays were strong now, the forest lit by beams of yellow and orange. The well-worn path we walked was littered with pine needles that crunched underfoot as we marched. Neither of us spoke for a while and the human silence was welcome. I let the sounds of the forest wash over me, feeling more relaxed and at peace than I had since being ripped from Annecy.

Grimal darted ahead of us. He seemed less alert than he had as we strolled through the town. Now, he looked as if he felt free. Running and leaping, he jumped from rock to rock and then launched himself over a large broken limb. I couldn't help but smile as I watched him. The forest had a positive effect on us both.

After walking for the better part of an hour, a crooked iron fence loomed ahead. The fence with sphere-topped finials stood perfectly straight in some sections and nearly falling in others, creating the look of a rollercoaster from afar.

The temperature seemed to grow colder the closer we walked. I wasn't sure if this was my imagination, but there was also a low mist hanging around the trees over our heads that wasn't there before.

Abigail pushed open the cemetery gate, hinges groaning with the effort, and stepped inside. By my count, there were only around a dozen graves in the small space, each different and unique. There were tall, ornately carved stones, smaller, more modest markers, and everything in between. The stones mirrored the fence. Some stood straight up and down, some tilted to one side.

"This is awfully far to be the town's cemetery," I remarked quietly to Abigail's back.

Abigail half-turned toward me. "Do you really think this is a resting place for them?" She threw back her head in a gesture that was meant to indicate the town behind us. "This is sacred ground for my kind. They don't even know it's here. The area is protected by a spell."

I glanced up at the fog. The mist and the cold made

sense now. It hadn't been my imagination. "How can I see it, then?"

Abigail turned to fully fix me in her stare. "Because I've allowed you to."

A small chill tingled down my spine and not from the cold. This was a good reminder that I wasn't really in control here. Abigail was. Thank the heavens she was on my side.

The witch spun back toward the gravestones, threading her way through them with quiet deliberation. I followed as quietly and carefully as I could.

Toward the back of the cemetery, she came to a stop, dropping down on her knees. The basket was set aside. Six rounded stones grouped together were all similar in one thing, the last names. My gaze roamed from one marker to the next.

Afton Allerton
Derian Allerton
Sybil Allerton
Mariam Allerton
Glenna Allerton

Abigail picked up a few pine needles and leaves from around the stones and tossed them away. From her pocket, she procured a small bundle of lavender. She pulled out six sprigs and then laid one in front of each grave as she whispered silent words. Grimal leaped up, perching himself atop Mariam's grave. As he sat, he licked his paw and cleaned his face.

"They think you are trouble," Abigail murmured.

Abigail still faced the graves, so I wasn't sure it was me she spoke to. She could have just as easily been speaking to the dead. In fact, I wouldn't have been surprised. When she didn't say anything else, I craned my neck, attempting to get a look at her face. "*They* think I'm trouble? As in, the people here?"

"They do. But they like you. So, that seals it."

I wanted to say *thank you* but wasn't sure where to direct the words. I bowed slightly, an awkward smile on my lips. "Thank you," I said to the back of Abigail's head.

Abigail whispered more words while I stood behind her, the mist swirling through the graves, raising chills on my arms. This was the perfect scene for a scary story. There was an absence of color here, as if everything was washed in gray.

Restlessness ached through my limbs. It was hard to be patient when all I wanted to do was act. I was afraid if I rushed Abigail or seemed ungrateful in any way, she would change her mind. I closed my eyes, focusing on my breathing to calm my mind.

After several more minutes, Abigail finally stood, brushing the graveyard dirt from the bottom of her dress.

"Why aren't there dates on the graves, Abigail?" I indicated the stones behind her.

She shrugged as she stuffed the leftover lavender back in her pocket. "It doesn't matter when they lived, only that they did."

This statement made sense to me. The name and the marker were really all that mattered. "Where to now?" I asked, hoping she would say it was time for the spell.

"Now, we pick some wild herbs from the forest." Abigail swept past me, out of the gray, dark cemetery, and out the gate, once again groaning on its hinges. For a moment, I hesitated, irritated by another delay. The farther Abigail moved away, the creepier it felt to stand amongst the dead all alone.

I jogged along, my jaw snapped shut to keep it quiet. Abigail already said she would help me. I didn't know the first thing about the witch's spells. If Abigail needed fresh herbs, then she needed fresh herbs. I would have to go along and trust in her process. Perhaps the herbs she intended to collect were needed for the spell to send me home.

Grimal must have grown weary. He no longer pranced

ahead of us, hopping from rock to rock. Now, he lagged, his tiny paws crunching leaves as he slowly padded across the forest floor.

Abigail walked south. I too, was growing weary. I didn't have preternatural stamina and the long walk was tiring. Add to that my need to eat again, and irritation began to rise. I didn't want to seem weaker than Abigail, so I did my best to keep up, sore though I was becoming.

After marching for what seemed like an eternity, I could remain silent no longer. "Will we be there soon?"

Abigail still held the lead. I knew she had to be an older woman and was struck by how unbothered she was. She came to a stop and turned to face me, a sour look on her face. "Human beings are so impatient." She sighed. "Yes, my dear, we are close. The meadow is right over that rise." Abigail pointed behind her. I saw the small hill and smiled with relief.

"Thank goodness. But, aren't you human?"

"I am and I'm not." Abigail whirled back around to continue the hike, like this explanation was all I needed.

I scrambled to keep up. "What does that mean? You're either human or you're not."

Abigail craned her neck to talk to me while she walked. "I'm human in that I'm mortal. And I'm not exactly human in that witches have longer life spans than non-magical humans, sometimes very long."

"How long?"

I heard Abigail sigh like a woman tired of questions from a pestering child. "It varies. Up to a couple hundred years."

I was surprised and now I had to know, rude or not. "Abigail, forgive me for asking, but curiosity has gotten the better of me. How old are you?"

Abigail snorted, her laugh echoing around me. "125."

"Get out," I blurted. Now my inability to tell her age made sense. Abigail was able to not only prolong her life, but also preserve her body. I was sure of it. Here was this woman, over one hundred years old, who could hike for hours in a forest when all I wanted to do was curl up with a pizza. I was impressed. I thought about Tash and wondered how old he was. I also wondered if Selene knew about this magic.

"You've surprised me in more ways than one, Abigail. I hope you keep on surprising me."

We reached the top of the hill. I was now too embarrassed to admit my exhaustion out loud, so I kept my relief to myself. The clearing before us looked like something out of a fairytale. It was covered in a deep-green clover, clumps of different plants growing all throughout. The plants and flowers cut through the green with a variety of blues, reds, and yellows. Bright rays of sunlight washed the scene in golden light. I wanted to sink down into the clover and fall into delicious sleep.

Abigail had other ideas. "Begin there, with the chamomile. Pick me ten flowers." Abigail pointed to a circle of white and yellow blooms. "When you have those, put them in the basket and pick ten sprigs of rosemary, there." She pointed to the bush of wild rosemary, its tangled branches reaching across the ground like long arms. Fresh floral notes and the earthiness of the herbs created the loveliest scent. I wanted to bottle this and take it home with me.

I did as I was told, picking first the chamomile and then the rosemary. When I finished, I deposited my herbs in the basket Abigail dropped in the center of the meadow. It was already filled with all manner of plants.

Abigail cleaned her hands on her skirt, fixing me in her stare. "I think we can put a spell together now."

CHAPTER THIRTEEN

Millicent

Clea was true to her word. We began with cards. Count Pierre and Countess Victoria Dubois, and the Viscount Gabriel Leclerq, joined me and Clea at one table. Across the room, Charles sat with Clea's husband and the Viscount Edgar Richmond and his wife, Alice. Charles's eyes were slits as he watched me like a serpent.

He hadn't said one word to me when I swept into the salon with Clea on my arm. I did my best to ignore him, instead focusing on the moment and the laughter of old friends. It was impossible to not think of what happened in the woods. Alexandre was gone off to find help, which left me at the mercy of that strange goddess. I knew she would reappear; it was only a matter of time.

The salon was all gilded finishes. The murals on the curved ceiling of Rubenesque ladies and chubby cherubs looked down at the room full of nobles in their silks and brocades. Crystal chandeliers provided all the candlelight we would need for the evening's festivities.

My gaze slid toward Charles. Why did he watch me so? His pompous look was almost more than I could bear. I squirmed a little in my seat. If I wanted to keep events in order, I would have to endure this. I just didn't know if I could.

I began to have wild thoughts. What if I veered off the path of my mortal life? So, what? Jack was the reincarnation of Julien; we already knew this. If I let Alexandre turn me, then turn Julien, what will it matter? They were the same, after all.

I shook my head to clear it of these images. No, they weren't the same. Jack and Julien looked like the same man, but Jack was different. He was who I loved; he was who I needed to return to. Being here in my old life, the stress of an uncertain future before me, was muddling my mind.

"Penny for your thoughts, my lady." Gabriel, who claimed the chair next to me, now leaned to the side, his voice low. I knew what he was about. This wasn't the first time Gabriel had tried his hand not only at cards but seduction.

I met his golden-brown gaze. "I was simply thinking about my lack of card-playing skill. What occupies you these days, Monsieur?"

He raised an eyebrow, his tongue darting past his lips to wet them. "Dreams of fair-haired maidens with black eyes."

Clea snorted across from me. "Oh, Gabriel. You should bark up another tree, you pretty boy."

With that, the whole table burst into loud laughter, including Gabriel, who held up his drink toward the Duchess with a wink. Gabriel downed his claret in one mouthful and then pushed back from the table with a flourish. "I demand dancing. What say you, our good hostess?" He bowed in front of me, the light-blue satin of his coat sparkling in the candlelight.

I looked at Charles, who shook his head.

"What a wonderful idea," I said, taking Gabriel's proffered hand and rising. I didn't care if I was supposed to be playing a role, I would never be subservient to any man again.

I avoided Charles's stare as Gabriel and I moved to the center of the room. The parlor was large and opulent. With only two small card tables set up at each side, there was plenty of space for the few couples here to dance to their hearts' content.

Since this was an impromptu performance, we had to rely on the musical abilities of two servants. One, the footman, played the violin and the other, a man I couldn't remember, accompanied him on the pianoforte, tucked away in the corner of the room.

"My dear." Gabriel bowed once more, his hand raised for me to take. Clea, her Duke, and the Count and Countess Dubois joined us.

The music began. We danced the minuet. I hadn't danced in so long, all other thoughts melted away as I concentrated. It was like riding a bike as the moves came back in an instant. I lost myself in the moment of music and movement, grateful to let go of the stress of my situation.

I could have danced all night. I began to feel more and more that my plan to veer off course would be a good one. Nephthys could try all she wanted; she wouldn't be able to keep me from my immortality. I could save Julien, who was also Jack, and everything would be perfect. Then I could go to Boston, find Annie, and change her. We could keep all the bad things from happening.

The music soared and with it, my hopes.

Until Charles put an end to all our fun. "That's enough!" he bellowed, his deep voice booming over the loud music.

The dancers all came to an abrupt stop and turned toward their host. It was clear to everyone's eyes how angry Charles was with his red, sweaty face.

"There was to be no dancing, tonight. Only cards and conversation."

We had upset his evening, me especially. I made eye contact with Clea, who immediately pushed her husband forward. The Duke swallowed, fidgeting with his fingers, as he said, "No need to be so hard, Charles. It was a bit of harmless fun." The Duke looked around, gesturing to those dancing to resume their seats. "Let's all sit now and carry on." He looked at me, a sympathetic smile on his face. I would be the one to face Charles's ire later in the evening.

My stomach dipped as I sat in my chair, held out for me by Gabriel.

"Well, it was fun while it lasted," he whispered as he pushed me in.

The room now felt awkward as everyone avoided everyone else. Clea shuffled the cards and dealt out another hand.

As I sat, staring down at the table, my breath became shallower and shallower. I wasn't afraid, I was angry. I didn't care what year it was. Who did Charles think he was, bossing us all about as he did? Even the Duke, who outranked him, wouldn't negate his friend, not in his own house. But, I would. I didn't care anymore.

My heart pounded furiously with purpose. I shoved my chair back so violently it fell over with a loud clang in the now-quiet room. Every eye at my table snapped in my direction. Let them stare. I hadn't been here for twenty-four hours and was already tired of it. I couldn't go back to being a woman led by men. Maybe I could teach these ladies a thing or two about standing up for themselves.

Clea's mouth gaped open. "Are you unwell, my dear?" she sputtered. Clea felt as I did, I knew, but there was social propriety to be adhered to.

All at once, I was suddenly calm, calmer than I'd been since I appeared in this dreadful chateau. Charles didn't scare me. "Yes, Clea, I'm quite well."

Charles strode across the room, his shoes clacking on the floor with each furious step. He grabbed my arm and whipped me toward him. My gaze penetrated his. I wouldn't look away and I wouldn't back down. "Millicent isn't well, at all. She's ill and will now say goodnight."

Gabriel moved to stand, a look of fury smattered across his face, but Charles pushed him back down. The man would only do so much to defend me. Charles was my husband, after all. I was nothing more than property. Good thing I didn't need Gabriel or anyone else.

"Enough." I wrenched my arm from Charles's grasp and stood my ground.

"Have you gone mad?" he whispered through clenched teeth. Charles balled up his fists at his side. I knew he wanted to hit me, but he had to keep some control, show some decorum. It was painfully hard for him not to reveal his true colors at this moment.

"No. I've gone sane. You can't tell me what to do, Charles. I am free of you. You disgust me and you've done nothing but disgust me every minute I've known you."

Gasps all around. I thought Charles may explode. His face was a dangerous bright red, drops of sweat beading at his temple. It was all he could do to keep from killing me. I was humiliating him in front of important guests; the Duke, most of all.

"Goodbye to you all." I would have liked to make a more dignified exit, but if I stayed any longer, Charles would have me locked up. So, rather than walk with my head held high, I sped from the room as fast as I could, hoping the shock of my words would keep Charles in place for a couple of minutes at least.

I ran to the front hall and pushed through the door like the house was on fire. When my feet hit the front step, I continued my flight, dragging up my skirts and dashing to the edge of the forest. I didn't dare look back. The men would come after me, Charles would give them no choice. He would deem me insane and have me sent away. All the sympathy would be his.

I thought of Clea. She alone would fight for me, but even her with all her connections, she wouldn't be able to save me from such a fate. The only person who could save me now was Alexandre. If he had already left on his journey, I was doomed. If they caught me, would Alexandre know where I was? Would he be able to free me of my torment?

Adrenaline rushed through me. My heart was thudding so hard, I was afraid it would burst. My lungs burned with the effort of my mad marathon.

By the time I slammed my body to a stop in the clearing before Alexandre's cabin, I had no breath and a sheen of sweat covered my body. "Alexandre," I called, my voice hoarse and dry.

The light was on inside. He was still here. I didn't want to cry, but unbidden tears streaked their way down my cheeks. I pressed on, moving up to the door and swinging it wide.

Alexandre was there, bent over his table, stuffing clothes inside a bag. His head snapped around, his blue eyes narrowed. "Millicent. Is that you or the goddess?"

"It's me. I need help." I rushed forward, stumbling on a loose floorboard and catching myself on the table ledge.

Alexandre moved around me, shutting the door and locking it. "Is it Nephthys?" He pushed back the window curtain to peer outside.

I collapsed in a chair, my limbs shaking with the effort of my run. "No, it's Charles."

"Your husband? What happened?" Alexandre moved back toward me, sinking down next to my chair.

"I couldn't stand it. I couldn't remain under his roof, under his rules. Oh, God." I moaned, dropping my face in my hands. "I've ruined it all. If only I'd kept everything the same. My future will be altered now."

"We don't know that, not yet." Alexandre scooped me up in his arms, his voice tender and sweet.

I pushed my hand against his chest, my heart still struggling to right itself. "Alexandre, I can't."

He laughed as he walked me over to the bed. "How horrible do you think I am?"

Pretty horrible, I thought.

"You're going to sleep and I'm going to protect you." Alexandre laid me down and then walked away. He was loving this. Me, helpless and needing shelter only he could provide. Alexandre was in heaven.

I propped myself up, terror winding its way through my heart. Alexandre was capable of mass slaughter. Ending the lives of those who came after me wouldn't even cause him to break a sweat. "Don't kill them, Alexandre. You must promise me. Don't kill any of them."

Alexandre turned around, his mouth pulled in a grimace. "Not even some of them?"

I shook my head. If I wasn't so weary, I would find his expression amusing. "No. They're all good people, all except Charles, but you can't even kill him, not now."

He shrugged, a look of disappointment on his face. "Fine. Stay in here, out of sight. If anyone comes snooping, I'll mesmerize them."

My shoulders relaxed and I realized how exhausted I was. "Perfect. Mesmerize all you like."

As much as I wanted to sleep, I didn't entirely trust Alexandre to keep his word. I sat, propped up against the headboard, listening intently to anything that may be occurring outside. After what seemed like an eternity, I heard voices in the clearing. The men were here, and they were talking to Alexandre.

I crept to the window, pushing the shade aside only so far to see as I crouched. The Duke, the Viscount Richmond, and Charles stood in a line in front of Alexandre who had his back to me. They seemed to be talking an awfully long time.

Just mesmerize them, Alexandre. I was fearful for the Duke. He didn't want to be here, I was sure. It seemed Gabriel and Pierre had refused to join my husband in seeking me out. I imagined Clea urged the Duke to go with them to ensure I wouldn't be harmed. He stood apart from the others, his face scrunched up in disagreement.

After the exchange of a few more words, the men turned around and left. Alexandre stood there until they were out of sight. I slunk to the floor, too tired to do anything else and my eyes closed.

As I lay on the uncomfortable, wood floor, exhausted to my core, my limbs began to shake. "What now?" I murmured. A fierce wind swept through the cabin, slamming me up against the wall. My stomach dove, my breath shallow from the force of the air against my face. I feared Nephthys was back to kill me this time, or perhaps she meant to suck me through time to another location.

I held my breath, trying to fight the cyclone with every ounce of strength I possessed. Fighting was pointless. She had me in her grip.

CHAPTER FOURTEEN

Annie

Abigail left her back door open. The breeze wafting in freshened the space and made me feel less claustrophobic. The witch stood over her butcher block, trimming the herbs we picked earlier in the day. Evening was already upon us— the hike through the mountains had sucked away precious hours.

Exhaustion lay in my arms and legs like dead weight. All I wanted to do was sleep. "How long will it take to prepare?" I asked through a yawn.

Abigail didn't look up as she answered, "A while yet. I need to eat first."

At the mention of food, my stomach growled. This human body was irritating, to say the least. I'd forgotten the almost constant maintenance one needed while alive. "I guess I do, too."

Abigail chuckled, motioning toward the larder with her head. "Bring out the cheese and bread. You can set the table while I finish here. And pour some cream for Grimal."

Grimal purred, moving around my feet as I worked. I pulled out a hunk of cheese and a dry loaf of bread, placing them on a platter in the center of the table. This was not the feast I was hoping for but would have to do.

I took a saucer from a shelf and filled it with cream for the cat. As I set the dish on the floor, he nuzzled my hand with the top of his head. It seemed he only liked me when I fed him.

Abigail and I sat down to our meager repast. There were a few coins in a little purse in my pocket which I intended to leave with her as payment for her assistance and for the food she provided. I felt I was draining her small supply of food.

The meal was eaten eagerly, dry or not. I munched on a piece of cheese. Rather than perking me up, the food was making me feel more tired. I didn't think such a thing was possible. "Thank you for feeding me, Abigail. I may need to lie down and close my eyes for a few minutes. Do we have the time?"

Abigail ate slowly, as if she had all the time in the world. "We have as much time as we want. Although, I know that isn't the answer you need to hear. It will take me at least another hour of puttering before I have my things ready. I'm slow and set in my ways. Anyway, it's best to wait until the witching hour to perform our spell. That will give us even more time." She looked up at me, her eyes unreadable. Abigail was an impossible woman to figure out. "You sleep until then. Grimal will watch over you while I make sure all is ready."

I was grateful to my core. There were at least three hours until midnight. I was sure a nap of that length would see me refreshed.

I wouldn't hear of Abigail cleaning up the table. She was doing enough for me, so I tidied while she went back to her task, even though my limbs were like anchors. When all was set to rights, Abigail pointed toward the door on the far side of the living area.

The bedroom was small but held all I would require. The single pine bed was old with a husk mattress laid over a net of rope. There was no feather mattress over the husk, only two blankets. One to serve as comfort under the body and one as a cover on top. This wasn't going to be cozy. I also didn't care.

I sank down into the rough fibers of the mattress, my eyes already closing. Grimal surprised me by hopping on top of my stomach and kneading me with his paws. Now that I had fed him, we were apparently friends. "How did you get in here? Go lay down." I picked up the cat, setting him gently on the floor. He stood there, staring at me. For a second, there seemed to be something behind his eyes I couldn't quite make out. In a moment, it was gone. That must have been the half of him that wasn't a cat. I wanted to learn more about familiars when I returned home. "I must be tired," I murmured, my head falling back as I drifted into unconsciousness.

There was chaos all around me. My sight was blurry, I rubbed my eyes hard with balled-up fists to try to clear them. There was a smell of wet rock in the air. I heard shouting, screaming. I shook my head, hard. When I finally had my bearings, I was in a stone room, a cave of sorts. It was dark and hard to see. Everyone was here; Mills, Alexandre, Thayer, Selene, Tash, and Jack.

I cried out and ran to Thayer, but something knocked me back. They were fighting. My old and new friends were battling something I couldn't see. Alexandre went down first, and Selene screamed. I tried to run to them. There was nothing I could do; I was rooted to my spot. Did they even see me?

Tash was bent over a mixture of blood and herbs. His mouth was moving, but I couldn't hear what he said. He was sweating profusely, his body wracked by tremors. A blast hit him, sending him flying backward into a huge black stone. He hit the stone with such force, he crumpled to the ground.

There was more screaming as I tried to move. I was frozen, pulling and pushing against whatever held me fast, desperately trying to get to my friends. Cement could not have held me faster. Tears streaked down my face; my mouth opened in a silent scream.

I bolted upright, my body drenched in sweat. It was a dream. My breathing was irregular, my heart hammering away in my chest. *Calm down, Annie. Calm down.* I closed my eyes, breathing deeply to ease the racing of my heart. I couldn't have been asleep for three hours. I cursed as I realized there would be no rest for me.

There was also no cave, only Abigail's bedroom blanketed in darkness. Grimal hopped onto my lap, causing me to jump for the second time. "Dammit, cat. Can't you see I'm trying to relax?" Maybe a familiar was something I didn't need after all.

Grimal ignored me, once again kneading my body, this time my thigh. "Why did you get so friendly all of a sudden?" The cat jumped from my lap to the floor. There was just enough light from the crack under the door to see him. Grimal crouched on his front legs and peered under the bed. Was he hunting or pointing? The childhood fear of monsters under the bed propelled me into action.

A chill crept its way down my arms. "What?" I whispered.

Without making a sound, I touched my feet to the floor then stepped away from the bed. When I was safely removed, I too crouched. I clamped a hand over my mouth, my heart pounding against my rib cage.

Grimal dipped his head. Light red hair splayed out on the pine floor beneath where I had lain. Abigail Allerton. I looked at Grimal and back at Abigail. I knew better than to scream.

A sound beyond the door alerted me to the presence of another. Grimal's head snapped up, his eyes narrowed into golden slits. He held a paw to his mouth in a universal gesture to remain quiet. If only he could speak, this would be so much easier.

"Annie, my dear one, are you awake?" Abigail's voice floated through the door. I didn't know what to do or what had occurred. Was the real Abigail dead all along or did this happen while I slept? There was no means of escape. The room was a box without windows. In order to get out of here, I would have to face whatever awaited me beyond and then work my way out the door.

I stared at Grimal, sympathy for his mistress burning a hole in my heart. "Stay with me. We'll get out of here, together."

Grimal nodded. I took a deep, shaky breath as I rose to my feet. The door swung open and there stood Abigail. I wiped my sweaty palms against my dress and affected a yawn. "Just woke up," I said. "Ready to begin?"

I tried to keep my face as natural as possible. I thought back to my days as a spy. That training would help me now. Whoever this was couldn't see me falter in any way.

Abigail's gaze shifted toward the bed, moved to Grimal, and then back to me. "Ready when you are," she said, her voice not quite the same.

I moved past her into the living area. It was imperative I get out of that room. There was only one person I could imagine this imposter to be. She must be the goddess of death, Nephthys. Who else could it be? I was powerless in my current form. What could I possibly do to escape? The only idea I had was to somehow distract her and run. Demeter still waited at the stables. If I could make it to her, maybe I could lose Nephthys for the time being. The sad little plan was all I had.

"You said we should do this in the meadow. Do we have everything we need?" This was a bit of a test. If Abigail had been murdered when I slept, then this woman would have no idea what I was talking about, hopefully going along with me and giving me the opportunity I needed to slip away. Abigail had said nothing about performing the spell in the meadow.

"Everything is prepared. I'll gather the items while you lead the way." Nephthys moved toward the butcher block and began stuffing herbs back in the basket. I was now convinced of her identity. She didn't mean to perform a spell. What she did intend, I couldn't guess, but she wouldn't be attempting to send me back. This goddess was not in her right mind.

"Of course," I said. I walked to the back door, Grimal at my heels.

The three of us moved into the alley, me in the front. My gaze darted every which way as I tried to puzzle out how I would do this. We walked silently through the dark streets. Instead of running ahead as he'd done before, Grimal stayed with me step for step.

As we neared the forest line, I realized it was now or never. If Nephthys lured us any further away from civilization, we were at her mercy. I felt intensely protective of Abigail's familiar.

Just as I was about to bolt to the right, a blast sent Nephthys barreling into me. I shoved her back and whirled around. Abigail, the real Abigail, stood in the dead center of the road with her head down. Her strawberry hair splayed around her as a soft glow emanated from her body. Grimal stood by her side. The cat was fast.

"Do you think it's that easy to kill a witch as old as I am? Goddess or not, let me assure you, it isn't."

My Abigail swung back her hands then flung them toward Nephthys, still in Abigail's form. It was crazy to watch these two identical women face off in the street. I dove out of the way as Nephthys was hit by another blast. The fake Abigail disappeared.

"Oh, thank the goddess, but not that one," I said, wincing as I stood. "What happened? Did she attack you while I was in the other room?"

"We can talk and move, come on." Abigail held out her hand, grasping my arm and pulling me back toward her house. "She appeared while you slept. Took me by surprise. I must have been knocked unconscious. When I woke, I reached out telepathically to Grimal. He told me where you were."

"I really need my own Grimal. Is she gone for good, do

you think?" I didn't imagine it would be so easy, but I sure hoped I was wrong.

"No. She'll regroup and hit us again. Which is why we need to get safe indoors. I can put up a pretty strong perimeter spell to keep her out." Abigail huffed as we walked. Her energy was clearly depleted, her shoulders slumped, and her gait was much slower than earlier.

"Abigail, thank you so much for all you've done. I can't apologize enough for the danger I've put you and Grimal in. I think it's best if I leave. Put up your perimeter, but I'm going to return to Boston."

We had reached Abigail's back door and she pulled me inside, slamming it behind her and throwing the bolt. "No chance I'll let you go off alone. This isn't your fault. I said I would help you and that's exactly what I'm going to do. I'm a witch of my word. Besides, this Egyptian goddess has now made me mad."

Abigail cleared off the butcher block. From her storefront, she grabbed all manner of jars. "Here, take these two and set them in the kitchen," she said, glass containers balanced in her hands.

Abigail pulled out a sprig here and a leaf there until she had a small mountain of herbs on her workspace. She pulled a knife from her pocket and sliced into her palm. I jumped, not expecting her to do that. If this was something she did often for spells, there was no indication of it. Her hands and arms were smooth and untouched. Witches must heal as vampires do.

As she recited an incantation, smoke began to billow from the sludge in front of her. Abigail swirled her hand in the air, picking up the smoke in her palm. I was astounded by the trick, watching with my mouth open.

She then walked around the perimeter of her little house, room by room until there was a ring of smoke throughout every space. I was impressed.

"We're locked in and more importantly, the goddess is locked out."

CHAPTER FIFTEEN

Alexandre

The location of the former Mirabeau Chateau was truly a spectacular place. Even though the chateau was long gone and the grounds were overgrown, you could see the appeal. The estate had been extensive. I remembered the gardens, statues, and gravel walks as my gaze swept the space around us. The land would be fun to restore, though I doubted Mills would ever want to.

It was the middle of the night, the half-moon and the cloudless sky providing plenty of light for those with preternatural senses and those used to the dark.

Tash sat on his knees. He had finished the locator spell to get a precise lock on the women and was now bent over the mortar and pestle, preparing the spell that would bind Annie and Millicent to his energy.

I watched as he wound a golden hair around his left arm and a dark hair around his right. Tash took a deep breath, turning his attention and his body to the center spell, the spell that would bring them back.

Tash inclined his head toward his daughter, who nodded. This was it. There was a crackle in the air from the previous magic. I wondered what effect the final, most difficult spell would have and if Nephthys would show her face. I looked around. The night was quiet, save for our odd little group.

Selene remained in the forest, hidden from my eyes. I held my breath as I watched Tash and Grace go about their work. If this wasn't successful, I didn't know what we would do.

Grace pointed one hand at Jack and Thayer, moving her arm in a small, circular motion. Electricity zapped from the tips of her fingers until there was a bright yellow circle of electrical energy drawn in the air by her small hand. I smelled burning metal, and the hairs on everyone's heads stood on end.

Continuing this motion, Grace pointed her other hand toward her father. She closed her eyes, unknown words rushing past her lips in a torrent. A current from the electric circle jumped into Grace's hand with a zap. She jumped but didn't stop. As I watched, the currents flowed through her, arm to arm. Grace flung her head back as the surge of electricity passed through her body and into Tash.

I watched with keen interest as Tash took a deep breath, the muscles and tendons of his neck flexing with new power. He took his ritual dagger in one hand, slicing into his palm, and let the blood flow into the mortar. A finger was dipped into this and used to draw something I couldn't quite see from my vantage point onto the gravel of the old drive. They appeared to be ancient symbols.

Tash then took this blood and poured it out into the center of these symbols. A dark smoke rose from the ground and he began to chant. The music of his voice was hypnotizing. After only a few seconds, I felt I was in a trance, dreamlike images blurring around the edges of my vision.

Small bolts of lightning hit the ground around them. Jack and Thayer, once sitting tall and strong, now slumped over as their energy was drained by Grace. A small flutter of concern moved through me as I saw them in this posture. This was new to all of us. We really had no idea if the spell would cause them lasting harm.

Something was happening. The air around us swirled as if a tornado were forming. I caught a glimpse of golden hair and cried out. I could just see the form of Millicent, materializing mere feet from me. I wanted to run to her and pull her fully into the present, but I was stuck in my place by the torrent of wind.

In a loud peel of thunder, Nephthys was there. She stood tall and beautiful, her gold net dress glinting in the moonlight. Under the sway of Tash's melodic chanting, I swayed on my feet. It took me several beats to realize this was the actual goddess standing in front of us. The others must have been entranced, as well. We were all frozen in a druglike stupor.

Then, everything happened too fast. Nephthys flung out her arms toward Tash. A fireball, large and flaming hot, appeared in her hand. "I'll end you, then I'll destroy the only means you have to ever get them back."

My head snapped from Nephthys to the streak my sister made as she bolted across the clearing. She never saw Selene coming. Selene pounded into her, knocking the goddess down hard into the rocky ground.

Tash dove to the side, the fireball hitting him in the arm as he fell out of the way. A scream tore through the night. It was from Tash, the burn to his arm a severe one. I rushed over to him, helpless to do anything but reach out a hand. Grace leaped forward, attempting to cover her father with her own small body. I pulled her off, wanting her to remain out of harm's way as much as possible.

Selene pulled her sword, positioning herself over Nephthys, who cackled once and disappeared. "Why won't she stay to fight?" The frustration was clear in Selene's voice. "Are there too many of us? Do we have her scared?"

Selene ran to Tash, tearing open her wrist and smearing the healing blood on his burn.

His breathing was ragged, but he was alive. Tash sucked in his breath as the blood hit his wounds, the skin repairing itself. I knew the feeling and it felt good.

Tash held on to Selene as he sat up. "She's not scared of us. That goddess is cunning, and she's preserving her energy. Every time she encounters us, we take a little more. She needs all she has to ensure she wins." Selene's blood not only sealed the wound, but it also gave him a surge of strength he desperately needed after the spell.

The spell. I saw Millicent in the rush of wind, I know I did. I bounced to my feet. Grace was fine, shaking her arms as if to wake them up as she kneeled behind her dad. Acting as a living conduit must feel strange. Thayer massaged his neck, moving it around in a circle. Jack crawled on his hands and knees toward a woman with blonde hair who lay on her side, turned away from us.

I wanted to push him out of the way and check on her myself. Rather than do this, I stayed put, watching now with everyone else as he turned her body toward him. Her hair spilled around her face, her eyes open and staring into his. Jack moaned some piteous puppy dog sound, pulling her into his arms and crushing her to his body.

They were back. We may not have finished off Nephthys, but at least the girls were home. I looked around for Annie. Thayer, after seeing the reunion behind him, was on his feet doing the same.

"Where's Annie?" I asked, looking down at Tash who still sat on the gravel like a stunned rabbit.

He didn't say anything. A frantic beating of my heart took over as I moved around the grounds. Thayer, too was searching, calling out her name. We moved parallel to each other, each covering half of the estate. There was no sign of her.

"I don't think she made it," Tash called out. He had finally rejoined us, standing up with the help of Selene.

Thayer stopped and staggered toward the witch. He stared down Tash in a way that made me fear for his safety.

"What do you mean she didn't make it?" Thayer's voice was raw with emotion.

"She isn't dead?" I blurted, my own emotion welling to the surface. My emotional tie to Millicent may have been stronger. I had been obsessively in love for two hundred years, after all, but Annie was equally as dear. The thought of losing her completely tore my heart in two. I gasped for air, tears threatening to fall. Despite this, I kept scanning the dark grass, hoping she may stir among the blades.

Tash held up his hands, moving toward Thayer. "She's not dead. Annie is still in the past. Nephthys interrupted me halfway through the final spell. Actually, we were lucky to get either of them back."

Thayer dropped the top half of his body, grasping his knees as he bent over. If he were human, I would say he was hyperventilating. As it was, his grief was simply overwhelming. To be so close to his love only to have her slip through his fingers was painful—it would be for anyone.

I wanted to comfort him, or maybe I wanted someone to comfort me. Instead, I remained where I was. This wasn't over and we still had work to do. "What did Nephthys mean when she said she would destroy our means? Was she talking about the dark star?"

Grace, holding hands with Selene, was the one to speak. "She had to be. Right, Dad?"

Tash nodded, a sad look on his face.

Millicent stepped into view, her yellow and white gown tattered around her legs. Seeing her dressed in this way brought back two lifetimes' worth of memories. "What's the dark star?"

Jack gripped her hand in both of his. "It's a magical stone in England that Tash used to heighten his spell. Without it, we wouldn't have been able to pull you forward through time."

Millicent's eyes went wide, her hair a wild tangle around her shoulders. "But what about Annie? Are you saying without this stone, she's stuck in the past?"

"That's right." Thayer's voice was quiet, broken.

Millicent pulled her hand free from Jack to gesture in the air as she talked. I passed a hand over my mouth to hide my smile. Mills could be an animated speaker when she got going. "When I was at the chateau, I had a nightmare. In the dream, we were all gathered around a black stone. We were fighting, maybe we were defending it."

Tash shoved his hands in the pockets of his jeans. "That's all well and good, but how do we all get there so quickly? Nephthys has the advantage in this."

"Does she know where it is?" Selene asked.

A collective shrug amongst the group indicated no one had the answer to this question.

"Then we have to try. I, for one, know I could never live with myself if we didn't." Selene looked to each one of us. We were all in agreement.

Mills rushed forward, throwing her arms around Selene. Selene stiffened for a moment then embraced her back. "Thank you." Mills pulled away, moving toward Tash, who she also pulled into a fierce hug. "Thank you for helping us. I would never have been set free if it wasn't for you. Annie would feel the same. Only, I'm a little confused."

My heel crunched gravel as I shifted my feet. "I'm pretty sure we're all confused."

Millicent really saw me for the first time. She smiled but didn't hug me. "Nothing seems to have changed in this time. But I didn't do anything I should have. The timeline, my timeline, should have changed."

Tash rubbed at his eyes with balled-up fists. This was a question he was best equipped to answer. "I wonder if you were in the actual past."

He had everyone's attention. Thayer moved closer into the circle. "What do you mean? Are you saying they weren't in the past at all?"

Tash shook his head. "Sort of. I think they were, and they weren't. All magical beings require energy. The energy needed to pull someone from the future and stick them back in the past, while also replacing them with the person they used to be, would take more vigor than I could possibly imagine. Nephthys is a goddess, yes, but she still must play by the rules of magic. I'm wondering if what she did instead, was place Millicent and Annie in a mirror of the past."

My gaze met my sister, who raised her eyebrows. I looked back at Mills. Life was so much simpler before magical creatures shattered everything I knew to be real.

"Okay, so Annie remains in a mirror of the past. Does that make it easier to bring her to us, especially now that you only have her to work on?" Jack spoke to Tash with his eyes never leaving Millicent. He seemed worried she would disappear again.

Tash nodded. "Actually, it does. I won't need to siphon energy. The hard part will be protecting the stone while performing the spell."

"Leave that to us." Selene nodded her head toward Mills, Thayer, and then Jack.

"I'm here, too." I shifted on my feet, not intending to sound childish and failing miserably. Would there ever be a time I would feel strong without thinking about my immortal strength? I had to keep reminding myself why I wanted to remain as I was.

"How do we get there?" Grace peered up at Selene as she asked the other question we were all thinking. Grace was a brave little girl. Her father must have been so proud, I knew I would be.

Tash knelt in front of his daughter. "You don't, I'm afraid. You're going back to the chateau, to be with Bria."

Grace opened her mouth to protest, but her dad silenced her with a hand. Grace slumped forward, likely knowing she couldn't argue. If he didn't need to siphon energy, her presence would be a liability. The grownups couldn't have any distractions.

Jack had hold of Millicent's hand again. "We are all depleted and none of us can walk on water. The only thing we can do is race to the train station, take it across the channel, and then race to wherever the stone is located."

"Agreed. If we can get on a train right away, the trip should take no more than two and a half hours. I'll run Grace home now." Selene gazed at Tash, waiting for the okay.

He scooped his daughter in his arms. "Be good and don't worry. We'll all be back before you know it."

There was silence from Grace. I wondered if she felt as we all did. This was far from over. Grace squeezed her dad fiercely around the neck, her eyes shut tight. If she was scared, she didn't show it.

Selene put Grace on her back and took off into the night. As we waited, I addressed Millicent for the first time. She had hooked her arm through Thayer's and stood in solidarity between him and Jack. To say I felt left out was an understatement. "Are you okay?"

Jack narrowed his eyes, turning his body so he half-shielded my progeny.

"It's fine, Jack." Mills took her hand out of his and slid her fingers behind Jack's neck, pulling him to her for a soft kiss on the lips. He relaxed by about half. "I'm so relieved to be back. There were a few scary moments, but some nice ones, too. I spent time with an old friend I missed very much. I told off Charles, which felt amazing. I also had a run-in with our Egyptian goddess."

Every head snapped in Millicent's direction. She had our full attention.

"It was weird. I really can't understand why she's doing all this. She appeared to me as I was returning from Alexandre's cabin."

Jack's body tensed. Millicent took his arm and continued. "She made it clear that she sees immortals as an abomination and will stop at nothing to keep us all mortal. Since we keep thwarting her, she may turn to killing us next."

"What happened? Did you escape her, or did she just

taunt you?" There was an edge to Jack's deep voice. He wanted to ask more about seeing me. I could read his irritation in the tautness of his body.

Mills slid her gaze toward me. "She was going to tell Charles I was sneaking out and have me locked in my room to keep Alexandre from changing me. Alexandre attacked and bit her. She disappeared."

I couldn't help but stand a little taller. "So, I saved you. Maybe I didn't have cause to be worried about how I would treat you. And, that was why I knew to bite her in the yard at Annecy. I had bitten her in the past—sort of."

Millicent's gaze fell to the ground. Something had happened. I wanted to prod, but she was clearly discomfited.

"I need to talk to you." Mills pulled Jack away from the others, his gaze like fire on mine before he turned to follow her.

I watched them as well as I could in the dark. I couldn't hear anything they said, but as far as I could tell, Jack's body language was one of a very angry man. As Millicent spoke, she worked her hands together, clearly nervous about something. She tried to take Jack's hand in hers, but he shoved them in his pockets instead. When they returned to the group, his arms were clasped tightly across his chest.

Millicent's face was crestfallen. I knew that look. She wore it whenever she was truly pained. I dearly wanted to know what they said, another pro in the column for immortality.

Selene sped up to us with a bundle in her hands. "Grace is safe at the chateau. I thought you'd want to change." Selene tossed the clothing to Mills.

"That's probably a good idea. Thanks." She sped off into the trees, returning moments later in jeans and a sweater. She still wore her eighteenth-century silk slippers.

Selene grinned. "I forgot shoes. But you're rocking that look. Are we ready?"

We were. There was no need to hang out any longer.

Again, Selene took me, and Thayer took Tash. Within minutes, we arrived at the train station in Paris.

CHAPTER SIXTEEN

Annie

The magical seal around Abigail's home would have to be a strong one to keep out Nephthys. Abigail and I sat at her table, Grimal perched on the tabletop between us, licking his paws like nothing had happened.

Abigail asked for silence so she could think through our problem. That was over an hour ago and my backside was getting sore. We were now two and a half hours from midnight, the moment Abigail said we should act. Patience was a challenge in the best of circumstances.

A tremble passed through my body. I thought I was cold, or perhaps needed more sleep, until another quake rocked me almost off the chair.

Abigail shot me a look, grabbing the table with both hands. Her eyes were wide with wonder, and her mouth open as if she were speaking although I couldn't hear a sound.

A blast of wind hit me full in the face, knocking me and the chair backward. I hit the ground hard, spinning around in the hurricane-force wind. My head throbbed from the forceful hit to the floorboards. I was completely powerless to stand or protect myself in any way. This was the same method Nephthys used to shove me through time. What was she up to now? So much for our protection spell.

I forced my eyes open. The strangest of images lay before me. "Thayer!" I tried to shout and reach out my arms, but the wind was too strong. Thayer sat on the bare ground with Jack and Grace, who was swirling lightning through the air with one hand.

Tash and Alexandre were also there. Tash bent over his witch's instruments with Alexandre lurking behind him. They were bringing me back. I had no idea how, but they were doing it. My only regret was I hadn't had the opportunity to say goodbye to Abigail and Grimal.

A flash of blonde hair whipped by me. "Mills!"

We were in France, the grounds of Millicent's old chateau spiraled by. The image became clearer and clearer as I began to feel stronger. Then, another flash of light and a sound like the crack of thunder. I fell back, tumbling through blackness.

"Annie, Annie. Wake up, girl." Abigail's voice sounded distant, but her hands were hard and insistent as she shook me.

A blinding flash exploded behind my eyes. Nausea moved through me. I rolled onto my side, pressing my forehead into the hard boards of the floor. "Water, please," I croaked. I tried to steady my breath.

Wood creaked as Abigail rose to her feet and padded away. Grimal pressed his cold nose into the side of my cheek, nudging me with affection. I appreciated the coolness of his wet nose. A moment later, Abigail hooked a strong arm around me, pulling me up into a sitting posture.

"Here." She pressed a cold glass into my hand.

The water was a life preserver. I clung to it, gulping down the contents. The liquid was partaken of too quickly. I sputtered, coughing some of it back into the glass.

"Slow down, child." Abigail took the cup from me. "You

have certainly caused me all manner of trouble," she huffed.

My head was clearing, so I opened my eyes. The few pieces of furniture in the small room were upset, lying at odd angles around the room. Candles from the two lamps had been blown to the ground and each one appeared broken in half, the effects of a strong wind blowing through a closed room.

"Abigail, I'm so sorry. I have some coins in my purse. It's all for you. I know what a terrible inconvenience I've been." I took the purse from my pocket and held it toward her.

Abigail waved her hand as she went about turning her meager furniture upright. "What inconvenience? Aside from almost being killed, all this isn't exactly valuable." She swept out her arm to indicate the room.

"If it's yours, it's valuable." I rose to my feet on shaky legs.

Abigail sat back in her chair. "I can't understand it. How could that woman have gotten through my defenses?"

"She didn't," I said, rubbing my now very sore backside. "It was Tash and Grace, and my friends."

"They were trying to rescue you. That makes more sense. I thought I felt a witch's signature." Abigail clasped her hands together on the table, a grin on her face.

"You look proud."

Her smile widened. "I am. Spells of this kind are complex; they take a lot of skill. What I don't understand is why it didn't work. You were gone. You know what they were doing, so you must have been there and saw them. How did it fail?"

"They were interrupted. That bit... I mean, Nephthys, interrupted them. I couldn't see what happened after that. I hope no one's hurt. Millicent was there, too." Fear wormed its way through my mind. I tried to remember everything I saw. After Nephthys showed up, I fell away and I couldn't see them anymore. It was impossible to know who was injured, or worse. My stomach churned with anxiety.

"Sit down, girl. Don't you get sick on my floor on top of everything else." Abigail kicked out my chair.

I shook my head. "I want this nightmare to come to an end." Even to my ears, I sounded whiny. I hated that, but I was so tired, so scared.

Grimal leaped onto my lap the moment I sat down. The purse was laid on the table and then I wrapped my arms around him, pressing him into my chest. He purred against me and the warmth was reassuring.

"It will, child. Your friends won't give up and neither will we." Abigail drummed her fingers on the table. "This is good information to have. If they tried once, they will try again. You and I will make sure we are ready for the next attempt. With my energy adding to the effort, the second time will work."

Anticipation welled inside me. I wanted to believe Abigail with all my heart. As I smiled at her, my eyes looked through her and saw Thayer slouching in the dirt. Something was happening to him and he looked tired. It was with great difficulty that he raised his head in the vortex. I wondered if he saw me.

Whether he saw me or not, I knew what he felt in the moment. He was aching to reach me as I longed to reach him. If only I could have grabbed hold of his strong arms. Would he have held me fast? Prevented me from falling away from them all?

Abigail continued to talk. I had to snap myself out of my reverie to hear what she said.

"It will be difficult to create the amount of energy we will require in my house. With all the fire I'll produce, we'll burn the place down. Although it will open us up to another attack, the most practical solution will be to relocate to the meadow." Abigail was stroking her chin as she spoke.

I really didn't want to go back out into the forest. I was more than a little spooked.

Abigail leaned back, her palms hitting the table. "No, we'll stay here. We can't risk it. In this house we are protected, out there, we're targets. Most of the energy will come from their side. I'll only be adding some of mine to help with the push. We'll clear the room."

"Are you sure, Abigail? I don't want any harm to come to you or Grimal." The cat had enough of my squeezing and pushed his body away from mine with his paws.

"I'm sure. I know you're tired, Annie, but there's no time to rest. Get up and help me move the furniture." Abigail spoke with parental authority.

I was tired, sleepy to my bones. Still, I pressed myself up, eager to get on with this and back to my heart.

Moving the few pieces of furniture didn't take long. We pushed the table into the bedroom and stacked the chairs in the kitchen. Less than a half an hour later, we were ready to begin.

Abigail took a piece of chalk and drew a large circle around the room. Inside the circle, she drew a myriad of other symbols. I only recognized the pentagram. She retrieved a wooden mortar and pestle and set this in the center of the circle along with her dagger and several small mounds of herbs.

A bundle of sage sat on the kitchen counter. One end of this she turned in the flame of a candle until a pungent smoke billowed forth. Abigail took her bundle and wafted it around the living area.

Preparing for a spell seemed to take an awfully long time. I stood back against a wall, worthless as Abigail went about her tasks. My eyes threatened to close with every breath I took, sleep trying its hardest to pull me under. I refused it, rubbing my eyes, massaging my arms, and moving from one foot to the other.

"I've done all I can do to prepare. Now we wait. Annie, come." Abigail knelt inside the circle, beckoning to me with one hand and pointing in front of her with the other. "You will lie here, over these symbols."

"If I lie down, I'll fall asleep."

Abigail smiled. "You needn't be conscious for the spell

to work. Perhaps when you wake, you'll be home."

I went to Abigail, taking her hand and tugging her up to face me. "I can't thank you enough for all you've done. Thank you, Abigail, and thank you, Grimal." I peered down at the cat winding his way around my ankles. "Tash and Grace will be so excited to learn about you."

Abigail encircled me in strong arms. It was impossible to believe this woman was over one hundred years old. "No thanks, necessary," she said into my ear. "Now, lie down. As soon as they begin their spell, we want to be ready."

I released my new friend and lay down on the floor, exactly as Abigail indicated. The boards were hard against my head and back. At this point, I could have slept on spikes and been comfortable.

Grimal curled up by my shoulder. The sleekness of his black fur was the last thing I saw before blacking out.

CHAPTER SEVENTEEN

Millicent

Jack hadn't spoken to or touched me since we left Burgundy. Granted, we really hadn't had an opportunity, racing through the countryside on our way to Paris. I intended to change this as soon as we were on the train.

Tickets were purchased by Thayer as the rest of us lolled around the station. The train we needed was in, and every one of us was eager to not miss it. There was a short line for tickets, even at this time of night. Thayer wasn't bothered, shouldering his way to the front. I thought he would be denied service, but one look at the giant German's face and the ticket clerk was happy to ignore his rudeness.

Thanks to Thayer, we made it onboard just as the train was ready to depart. Now that we were all here, the others could do what they'd like. I grasped Jack's hand, pulling him through car after car, into a bathroom where we could be alone.

I pushed him back against the sink and closed the door behind me. "Okay. Are you going to talk to me or continue to fume?"

"I'd like to fume for at least another hour." Jack said this with a straight face, so I did my best not to smile.

I stepped forward until our toes were touching and slid my hands over his chest. "You can fume for as long as you like. I'm just thrilled to be home with you. I was so scared, Jack. You've no idea. I'm sorry for canoodling with Alexandre. I was terrified, confused, and all I wanted was to get right here."

I picked up his arms and clapped them behind my back. The tension in Jack's body released. He pressed his arms around me, crushing me to his chest. My head laid against his shoulder.

"I thought I was going to lose my mind. I'm not mad at you. I'll never like Alexandre, never, but I understand why you did what you did. I'm thankful to him for one thing; he protected you. Let's not talk about him anymore. I'm just so grateful to have you back," he murmured into my hair.

"I'm grateful, too. We must do everything in our power to get Annie home, Jack. I'm scared for her." My voice broke. I had to keep the tears at bay. Bloody streaks were hard to hide, and we still had the rest of the train ride.

"We will. I know what Thayer's feeling. It's the worst, most painful heartache."

I pulled back to kiss Jack. We kissed often, and yet I never failed to feel a thrill through my body at the press of his mouth against mine. His lips were warm, soft, and yielding. We touched and tasted for a minute too long, desire taking hold of both of us. We knew what we had to do.

Jack spun me around, sitting me up on the sink. I leaned back as Jack pulled off my jeans. A bathroom sink on a train was probably the most unsanitary place I'd ever had sex, but it also felt a little naughty.

I thought we would probably get right to it, but Jack had other plans. After pulling off my jeans, he took hold of my foot and arched my leg up in the air. He pressed his warm mouth against the instep of my foot, kissing and licking his way up my leg. The sensation drove me wild. By the time his tongue was playing with the delicate skin inside my knee, I saw stars burst behind my eyelids.

There was no one else I would rather play with, no one else who could make me feel what this man did. I would pass through a thousand lifetimes to reach him again and again.

I gripped the counter with both hands as he continued his way up my thigh at a maddeningly slow pace. By the time he pushed my panties to the side with his tongue, I had to bite my lip to keep from moaning too loudly.

My hands gripped the back of his head, waves of pleasure rolling through my body as Jack sucked and teased. My climax rocked me to my core. I had to be careful not to break the glass behind me with my head.

Jack stood, wrapping his hands around my buttocks and pulling me onto him. He pressed into me over and over, our bodies close, our mouths tasting, until once again, I saw the heavens open.

We found the others taking up three rows of seats. Selene and Tash sat in one row, Tash sleeping soundly against Selene's shoulder. She looked up, a soft smile playing on her lips as we passed. Behind them was Alexandre. He reclined across an entire row, his back against the window and his feet dangling into the aisle.

At first glance, Alexandre appeared as any casual male, but I could see the exhaustion; the redness in his eyes and the sallow yellow tint to his skin. He raised an eyebrow as we passed. "Where have you two been?"

Jack, walking ahead of me, stopped. He would love to lay into Alexandre. I pushed him forward. "Go sit with Thayer. I'll be right there."

Jack glanced back at me, a wry twist to his mouth, but he continued to the next row where Thayer sat, straight and still. Jack shot me one last look before dropping into a seat next to his friend who continued gazing out the window.

I winked at Jack before settling myself across from

Alexandre. "How are you holding up?" I asked. I knew Alexandre and I needed to exchange words; I just didn't know what those words should be.

He shrugged, his cool demeanor in place, but his eyes hollow from exhaustion. "I'm better by about fifty percent. Once we get Annie, I'll be able to fully breathe again."

I nodded, chewing a bit on my bottom lip. "We all will." My gaze penetrated his. "You need to sleep. Take a cue from Tash and close your eyes. When was the last time you slept for a full night?"

"The night before Annie, Thayer, and Jack came to me in Ireland."

I looked at him quizzically. As far as I knew, I'd been gone less than a day. When I came to in Mirabeau Chateau, it was daytime. I was pulled back later that very night. "How long was I gone?"

"Five days. Why? How long did it seem to you?" Alexandre sat up, dropping his feet on the ground. Thayer and Jack peered over the back of the seats. Selene was behind me, and wouldn't want to wake Tash, but I knew she could hear us.

"Less than twenty-four hours."

A wrinkle appeared in Alexandre's brow. "Strange. Time must be different in the mirror, slower. That's probably a good thing."

My gaze slid to my hands. It was a good thing. If I'd had to endure five days in the past, who knew what would have happened. This gave me more hope where Annie was concerned. She was likely experiencing the same slowing effect.

"Thank you, Alexandre." My voice was soft, muted.

Alexandre dipped his head down to look me in the face. "What are you thanking me for?"

"Thank you for always being there for me. I don't think I was always very fair to you. I think I used you and probably manipulated you a little, too. You were the most consistent part of my life for a long time, and you deserved better." I leaned back against the seat. "I'm not saying you didn't royally screw up. You did some horrible things."

Alexandre's face was the softest I'd ever seen it. His sea-blue eyes were calm, his body language relaxed as he leaned over with his forearms resting on his knees. "Some of those things will haunt me until the day I die. I appreciate what you've said, Mills. Your words mean a lot."

"Tell me about Bria. I want to know everything about her."

The train stopped in London where we all departed. The hour was very late, the streets busy regardless. London was lights, people, and activity. There was no time to play. We had to get to the dark star without any further delay.

I never thought to ask where exactly we were going. For some reason, I envisioned the dark star to be near the site of Stonehenge. In my mind, this made perfect sense. But this wasn't at all where we were headed.

We took a cab away from the city, the driver giving us the most bizarre looks as he deposited the six of us off in the middle of nowhere. As the car drove away, the headlights becoming dimmer and dimmer as it traveled down the lonely road, Tash took charge.

"We're going north to Bakewell. It's about three and a half hours by car. How long do you think the journey will take us?"

I pulled my hair back, wrapping it an elastic procured at the train station. "Minutes. It isn't much farther than Annecy from my old chateau."

Tash handed his backpack to Jack. "Perfect."

Bakewell was a town full of charm, a place out of a fairytale. Stone cottages, quaint churches, and greenery of all kinds surrounded us. We moved quickly through winding streets, silent as our heads moved all around to take in the sights. Tash and Alexandre now walked as we were nearing our destination. Tash wasn't exactly sure of the stone's location. He was following some sort of energy signature only he could feel.

"I'm going to need a weekend here, soon," I said as I gazed into passing shop windows.

Every now and then, Tash would stop, close his eyes, and change direction. Every time this happened, Thayer clenched his fists at his sides. I, too, was beginning to feel more and more anxious.

After we had walked almost the entire length of the town, Tash spun around on his boot heel. "It's close." He whipped back around and took off at a run out of town and into a copse of trees. We all followed suit.

We ran up an emerald-green hill. About halfway up, Tash stopped, dropping his head and catching his breath. "I think what we're looking for is at the top, but I'm spent," he said between gasps of air.

"Me, too." Alexandre was taking up the rear, also breathing dangerously hard.

"Hop on," I said to Alexandre.

Selene took Tash and we sped to the top. The peak was breathtaking. I deposited Alexandre and stared at the scenery. Below us stretched the town. The hillside was covered in green moss and purple heather. Large stones jutted out at various angles, creating the look of steps built for giants.

"Over here," Tash shouted behind me. He was standing in front of what looked to be a large solid rock. Tash laid his hand over the face of the stone and said something I couldn't understand. The rock face wobbled as if an illusion, then disappeared, revealing a cave within.

"Whoa." I was astounded. Never had I seen anything like this. I looked to Jack and Thayer, both of whom stood with their mouths open.

"It takes a minute to get used to." Alexandre was watching my face, a grin spread out all over his.

"Is this the kind of thing you do, now?" I asked him.

"You don't even know the half of it." Alexandre raised

his eyebrow as his sister snorted a laugh. I was impressed. Alexandre had been up to a lot more than I realized.

Tash and Selene entered the opening first, Selene leading the way. The interior was dark, so dark that Alexandre stumbled and fell into Jack after only a few feet. "I hate caves," Alexandre grumbled.

I expected Jack to shove Alexandre off, but he didn't. Jack simply waited until Alexandre had righted himself then pressed on.

"Here." Tash fished around his pack, pulling out two small tactical flashlights. He passed one to Alexandre then continued ahead. The rock was cold, and water trickled here and there down the walls, giving off a petrichor-like scent.

We didn't have far to walk until the cave opened into a living-room-size cavern. The surrounding stone was gray with a faint glint of veiny silver that sparkled in the light of the illumination. In the center sat the largest geode I had ever seen. This was the dark star, a huge stone of raw black opal. It was mesmerizing. I could now feel the energy of it. It hummed, buzzed with power.

The air was electric, and every fine hair of my body stood on end. I gaped at the stone. "This is incredible. How did it get here?"

Tash pulled out his instruments as he answered. "No clue. It's a mystery, even to me."

All I could do was shake my head. I was tempted to reach out and run my fingers over the surface, but something told me maybe I shouldn't. Instead, I stood back along the edge in between Jack and Thayer. On the other side stood Selene and Alexandre.

Selene looked down at Tash. "What can we do?"

Tash drew a circle in front of the opal in chalk. "Nothing. It won't take me long to get all this ready. The stone is going to be the catalyst for me this time. Being in such proximity, the power will be great."

"What about Nephthys?" Thayer stepped a half an inch forward, his face turned back toward the opening of the cave.

"If she shows up, stop her." Tash was ready to get this over with. His short, matter-of-fact sentences made this clear. We were all ready.

He drew several symbols inside his circle with a practiced hand. Tash pulled out a mortar and pestle, grounding what I assumed to be herbs inside the bowl. "Here we go," he said. Tash hauled out a dagger and cut into the palm of his hand. I was enthralled, watching everything he did with rapt concentration.

The blood oozed into the mortar and smoke tumbled out. Tash poured this substance into the center of his circle, chanting words as he did so. The air sparked around him. It more than sparked, lightning flashed.

Jack put up his arm to hold me back. I realized I had stepped forward a little too far, fascinated as I was.

There was a commotion toward the mouth of the cave. Selene sped off. I realized Nephthys must be there. A moment later, Selene flew past us, over Tash. His head snapped around to see if she was okay.

"Don't stop!" I yelled as Nephthys came into view. She looked different. Before, she appeared as rather an ordinary woman, aside from her clothing. Now, she glowed like fire. I moved in front of her, my fangs bared, ready to pounce.

"Millicent, no." Jack tried to push me out of the way, but I stood firm. This woman was the cause of all our pain. I rushed at her, determined to pounce. The moment I hit her, I was flung off in the same manner as Selene.

I flew through the air, spasms wracking my body, and slammed into the stone wall behind the dark star. Selene was nowhere to be seen. My head screamed with pain as I attempted to scramble to my feet. My stomach took a dive as I realized we were all in mortal danger.

There was more shouting and a loud, piercing scream that shook me to my core.

"Millicent." Alexandre was there, pulling me up to my feet. I slapped my face to clear my head and moved around the opal with all the speed I could muster. What I saw stopped me dead in my tracks.

Thayer and Jack both lay unconscious on opposite sides of the cave. They must have rushed the goddess and also been flung against the stone walls. Nephthys had Selene by the throat with one hand and was pointing at Tash with the other. From that hand emanated a stream of fire aimed directly at the witch's heart.

Tash, however, was not giving up. He also glowed, not as powerfully as Nephthys, but he was lit with power. The hum of the dark star became louder and louder. Tash flexed as a surge of some unseen force from the opal moved into his body. His eyes were wild, his body covered in a sheen of sweat, his fists clenched as he held them out to the side.

I stood back, holding Alexandre behind me. There was nothing I could do but watch. If Tash couldn't save us now, we were all doomed.

The dark star began to tremble, the loud buzzing reverberating off the stone. Alexandre clamped his hands over his human ears to protect them from the brain-splitting sound. I didn't think the stone could take much more. If it exploded, Alexandre and Tash would die, and I wasn't so certain about the rest of us.

When the walls of the cave began to shake along with the stone, I knew death was imminent. I would cover Alexandre's body with my own, but who would protect Tash? It was inevitable someone would perish. I pressed Alexandre further behind me as if this could shield him.

Bits of stone started falling from the ceiling. This was it. The structure could only handle so much friction. All the while, Nephthys aimed her blast of fire at Tash. How long could he hold out, dark star or not?

As if in answer to my question, Tash flung his hands toward the goddess, unclenching his fists as he did so. His own blasts, twice as strong as the goddess's, hit her in the face and chest. Nephthys stumbled back, trying with all her might to hold her ground.

Selene struggled, kicking at the goddess while clutching with both hands at the hand that held her fast. Selene's struggle increased. Nephthys must have been bearing down on her in a last-ditch effort. There was still nothing I could do but watch. If I tried to cross the streams, I could be incinerated by the fire these two flung at each other.

A crack shot down the ceiling of the cave over our heads. Across from me, Jack stirred. *Stay where you are,* I thought. Thayer, too, was beginning to wake.

A loud pop and flash of light knocked me into Alexandre, who I had pressed between my back and the rock wall. A bolt of lightning jumped from the dark star and into Tash. He stumbled forward then screamed a primal yell. The light bursting from the palms of his hands hit Nephthys in one final burst.

Selene fell hard to the floor, scrambling away, as Nephthys's fire died. The goddess now stood without her glow, as she had appeared to me in the forest outside my chateau.

A flash of auburn hair behind her alerted me to the presence of Annie. Annie launched herself at Nephthys, sinking her fangs into the goddess's shoulder. Annie pulled her down to the ground as she drank and drank. Nephthys was helpless. She closed her eyes as Annie swallowed. Selene and I pounced next, each of us sinking our fangs into the goddess's tender flesh.

The energy in the cave changed again and I looked up to see an opening of some kind between us and the dark star.

"Throw her in," Selene said, through the haze of the blood.

The three of us picked up Nephthys, hauling her through the strange portal. She disappeared.

"What happened to her?" Annie looked up at us, a trickle of blood dripping down her chin.

Selene rubbed her throat, staring at the spot Nephthys occupied only a moment ago. "She's gone, back to where she belongs in the hell dimension."

Annie smiled, a smart-alec comment likely forming in her mind. Before she could release her quip, Tash fell to the ground in a heap.

Selene crawled to him, pulling him up in her arms. We all gathered around. Annie and Thayer, with arms clasped around each other, would have to wait for their reunion.

Tash was barely breathing, his pulse a thread at best. Selene stroked his cheek, blood tears dripping onto his face.

Mills reached out a hand, placing it on Tash's arm. "Change him, Selene."

Annie stiffened, her steady gaze trained on Tash's face. "His ancestor made me promise we wouldn't change him. I can't go against her wishes. She was adamant."

Mills looked up, a sad smile on her lips. "I'm not sure what you mean, but it's not our choice, Annie. It's for Selene and Tash to decide."

The furrow forming between Annie's brows told me she didn't think it was up to anyone but Tash. "His ancestor said the blood would turn him evil." I wondered what she meant by Tash's ancestor. Had she met another witch during her foray into the past?

Selene shook her head. "Annie's right. He doesn't want to be like us. His coven will hunt him down, kill him for what he is."

"Then we'll protect him. He's one of us, now." Thayer tightened his arm around Annie's shoulder.

Selene gazed down into Tash's face. "It has to be your choice. Say the word and I'll do it," she whispered.

It felt like we all held our breath as we waited for an answer from Tash. I wasn't sure he could give one. His lids were half-closed, his breathing raspy and irregular. "Do it," gasped Tash. "Do it for Grace."

In my mind, I heard the sobbing of the little girl from my dream. She must be Grace. Selene didn't need to be told twice. She pushed his head to the side, sinking her teeth into the flesh of his neck.

Jack tapped me on the shoulder, holding out his hand

for me to take. I followed him out of the cave, the others not far behind. This was an intimate act for them alone. Whatever Tash faced, Thayer was right—we would protect him.

Outside, the night was one of serene simplicity. The stars shined overhead, the breeze wafted the grass and heather. I was never so happy to be out in the open. The terror I experienced in that cave wouldn't be soon forgotten.

Annie threw her arms around me, surprising me from behind. "Do we have a lot to talk about."

I turned to return her embrace. "Tons. We have all the time in the world for that. Go kiss your soldier. He's missed you."

I released my best friend and she bounced off toward Thayer, his eyes crinkled at the corners in his delight. I swear, he only ever smiled at her. Alexandre collapsed onto a boulder, exhaustion written in every muscle and line of his face. "Just say the word, Alexandre. I know you want it back."

Alexandre looked up at me. "Right now, I want to sleep." He smiled, gazing up at the brilliant dark sky. "I do want it back, but Bria has to want it, too. I'll let you know, after the baby comes."

Alexandre with a baby wasn't something I ever thought I'd see. I tried to imagine him changing diapers and pushing a baby stroller. All I came up with were images of Alexandre throwing up that eyebrow as he hit on woman after woman.

When Tash and Selene walked out of the cave, the change in Tash was immediately obvious. His eyes glowed with preternatural life, his body, muscular before, was even more so, now. We owed him more than we could ever repay.

CHAPTER EIGHTEEN

Annie

The kitchen in Annecy was a strange place for us to gather. Even though none of us ate, we always found ourselves in this room at one time or another. I sat at the pedestal table with Thayer and Tash, now a newly formed vampire. He was transitioning well, his only worry for Grace.

"When the coven comes after me, Grace will be alone in the world." Tash massaged the back of his neck, foot tapping against the chair leg.

I reached out a hand, wrapping my fingers around his forearm. "You're assuming a lot. We don't know if they'll come, and if they do, they'll have quite a fight on their hands. I imagine they won't want that. And one thing you can count on from here on out is that Grace will never be alone, again. She has seven people, besides you, who will always have her back."

Tash smiled. "Thank you. You don't know what it means to me to hear you say that."

"You'll never have to thank any of us for anything. We all owe you—big time. And you're not the only one I owe."

Tash looked at me, quizzically.

I leaned back in the chair, ready to tell Tash all about Abigail. "I also owe your ancestor. Her name was Abigail Allerton."

Tash moved his head back, eyes widening in disbelief. "You met Abigail?"

"I did. She's really something. In fact, she may be the most interesting person I've ever met. She and her familiar, a black cat by the name of Grimal." I turned to Thayer. "By the way, I want a familiar now."

Tash laughed. "That's incredible, Annie. I've heard amazing stories about Abigail. She was a very powerful witch. She lived to be two hundred years old."

I was comforted in the fact that Abigail was remembered by her descendants and that she had lived a long life. "About that. Are you super old, too?"

Tash laughed. "Super old in that I'm middle-aged. But I haven't started preserving myself yet, if that's what you're asking."

"What about what Abigail said about the blood turning you evil?" I had to know if we would one day be facing Tash the villain.

Tash passed a hand over his mouth in thought. "I'm not sure. I don't feel like I want to slaughter the masses. I guess only time will tell."

The thought of having to put him down one day was not a pleasant one, so I changed the subject. "Whatever happened to Abigail's familiar, Grimal?" I asked.

"He went with her. That's how it works. Witches and their familiars are bound together. When the witch dies, so does the familiar."

This news caused conflicting feelings. It was nice to know Abigail hadn't departed the world alone, but what if Grimal wasn't ready to move on? He wouldn't have a choice. I imagined that without his mistress, his life wouldn't be the same.

"If you really want a familiar, I can help you with that.

I've never known a vampire to have one, but that doesn't mean we can't give it a try."

"Really?" I perked up at the thought. What sort of animal would I choose if I could? I thought an owl would be just my sort of creature, a familiar who could keep up with me as I danced among the treetops.

Selene walked into the room. "Can I crash the party?"

Tash pushed out a chair for her. Selene smiled warmly at us. "I've been thinking about my tarot cards. It seems they came true, after all."

She grasped Tash's hand. He nodded, a strange look on his face. "The death card, it was about me. I was the metamorphosis."

There was much for me to learn about his world. "What are we talking about?"

Selene smiled, her gaze meeting mine. "Tash took me to have my cards read in Romania. They were bleak, downright terrible. But, all in all, I'd say we ended up okay. Tash may disagree."

Tash rubbed a hand over his goatee. "I'm fine with it. The only person I truly worry about is Grace. But she's resilient and I'll be able to protect her all the better now. Plus, this gives me more incentive to find a cure for this vampire madness you all seem to face."

Selene gave his hand a hard squeeze. "We would all appreciate that. There's something else we need to discuss." Selene paused. "I've been contacted about some trouble in Russia. A maruda is accosting babies in their cradles. Feel like hunting a demon with me? Grace said she's in." Selene was talking to Tash, but my senses perked up. Hunting demons sounded like a cause I could get behind.

My gaze slid to Thayer, who was shaking his head. "What? You don't know what I'm thinking."

"Yes, I do, Annie Monroe. No demons." Thayer continued shaking his head as if this would help him make his point.

"Are you interested, Annie?" Selene leaned further over

the table, looking between Thayer and me.

"Very. I need something to do, something important. I'm not good at playing house." I patted Thayer's hand as I spoke to Selene.

She chuckled, her eyes crinkling with her laughter. "I think you'd be uniquely suited to the work. We'd be happy to have you and Thayer come with us. The more the merrier."

"Wait a minute." Tash held up his hands. "I didn't say yes. Grace needs to go back to school. She can't traipse around the world fighting demons."

Selene waved her hand around. "Grace and I took care of that before she went to bed. There's this new thing out there called online school. Besides, you and I both know that Grace isn't a sit-in-a-classroom type of girl."

Tash pulled a face, his eyes narrowing in mock anger. "Nice of you two to fill me in."

Selene picked up his hand, dropping a kiss on his knuckles. "You're welcome."

I ran my fingers back through my hair, wondering if I should cut it short like Selene's. "Wait, what is this?" I pulled a section of hair as far as I could in front of my eye. A good-size lock was missing. "That bitch took my hair."

Tash laughed so loud, I thought he might injure himself. "Don't worry, Annie. Abigail won't do you any harm."

After it was decided that the five of us would leave following Alexandre's big announcement, I went outside in search of Mills. She and Jack were lounging on a chaise meant for one. "Before I interrupt something more important, I wanted to say a preemptory goodbye."

Mills sprang off Jack's lap to stand in front of me with her hands on her hips. "Where do you think you're going?"

I laughed, pulling her into my arms. "Thayer and I are going with Selene to fight demons in Russia."

"Of course, you are," she said against my hair. She released me, her hands still on my shoulders. "That sounds like the perfect occupation for you."

"That's funny, Selene said the same thing."

"You're a rebel who needs a cause, my love, I've always said so. Just make sure you come back and see me in between relocations." Her face was soft, her black eyes clear. Mills was once again exactly where she should be, at home with her love.

Leaving Mills was always hard, but the sweet reunions also made the goodbyes worth the pain they caused. "I'll come back so often, you'll be sick of me."

CHAPTER NINETEEN

Alexandre

The moment we arrived back in Annecy, I slipped into bed with Bria and slept. I could have slept for days if Bria hadn't shaken me awake at dusk. "The vamps will be up soon. I thought you'd want to see them. Selene and Tash are leaving."

"They can't go yet." I sat up, rubbing the sleep from my eyes. I had plans, and if they all left, they would be spoiled.

"I'm pretty sure they can go whenever they want, Alexandre." Bria was moving around the room, pulling clothes out of drawers and throwing them without being folded into a suitcase. "I'm ready to get home myself."

"We'll go home after we get married."

Bria spun around, her red hair slapping her in the face. "When are we getting married?"

"Tonight." I had the license tucked away in my pack. It was procured before Mills went missing. Before Selene left for Paris, I told her to get herself ordained online. My initial plan was to have my sister marry us when she returned from Transylvania. When, I wasn't exactly sure, there hadn't been any rush and with Bria so sick, I knew she wouldn't want to anyway. Now that she was well and we were all gathered, this seemed to me the perfect time.

I whispered to Mills before I went to bed that I would like to have the ceremony in her back yard. She told me to leave it all to her, as I figured she would. We had everything we needed.

The evening was going to go off without a hitch, or so I hoped. Mills told me to stay inside while she and the others decorated. I was having a hard time sitting still as I waited. Bria was upstairs with Selene getting dressed and I sat alone in the living room in a perfectly fitted tuxedo. Millicent was a master of procurement.

At midnight, I strolled out the back door. The lawn looked like a wonderland. Candlelit lanterns hanging from poles dotted around the grass cast a soft, romantic light. Candles floated on the surface of the small lake, extending the stunning effect. A white runner began at the foot of the stone steps and stopped in front of a white arbor covered in blood-red roses.

The scene was simple yet the loveliest I'd ever beheld. Millicent was fussing with the arbor, tucking a stray rose back into place. I was touched by the effort she went to in order to give me and Bria an exquisite wedding.

"Mills, it's perfect. Thank you."

She finished her task, her black gaze sliding toward me. "Alexandre in a tux never fails to impress." She looked around. "Don't tell Jack I said that."

I laughed. We were alone, the others having gone inside to change clothes. Mills stepped forward and wrapped her arms around me. I buried my face in her lavender-scented hair as emotions swept through me. We stood, embracing for a moment longer, neither of us speaking. I was afraid if I spoke, the tears forming on the surface of my eyes would break free.

Millicent broke the hug, taking a step back, her hands still clasping my shoulders. "Against my better judgment, I'll always love you, Alexandre. You're my friend, my brother."

This was more than I thought to ever hear from her lips and I was grateful for it. "Same…except for the better judgment part."

Mills laughed, tossing her golden hair. "I better rush off. Time to slip on a dress. Strange, I know."

She skipped off. I smiled, watching her go. Mills was all about her jeans. You knew it was a special occasion when she wore a dress.

There was nowhere to sit, so I milled about the lawn. Butterflies descended upon my stomach as I strolled. I, Alexandre, was about to be married. The world had changed, indeed. There was no other woman better suited for me than Bria. She was my match in all ways. The love I felt for her dwarfed any feeling I'd ever had for anyone. Living my life with her, raising our child, was everything I wanted.

Selene cleared her throat, drawing me from my thoughts. "Don't you look handsome, Caesarion."

I turned. Selene looked gorgeous. She wore a golden silk batwing-style dress that complemented the warmth of her skin. Around her wrist, she wore Cleopatra's gold snake bracelet and on her index finger, the lapis scarab ring. In her hand, she held a notebook containing our vows.

"You could be her, Selene." Our mother shone through Selene's eyes. I remembered Cleopatra, her fire and her heart. She would never have an equal, but my sister was as close as this world would see.

Selene smiled, looking down at the bracelet. "She's with us. They all are. Are you ready for this?"

I nodded. "More than ready."

Tash and Grace came out next, Grace pulling Tash by the hand. She wore a pale-pink dress with a tulle bottom that floated around her as she walked. She looked like a princess, her dark hair topped with a tiny, glittering tiara. In her hand, she clutched a basket, filled to nearly overflowing with red rose petals. Tash, in a tux, as all the men would be, would walk Bria down the aisle.

Next came Annie and Thayer. Annie requested to stand up with Bria, and she looked lovely in a long-sleeved red velvet gown. She bounded up to me, her eyes shining, and threw her arms around me. I wasn't used to all this love from my progeny. If we didn't get on with this, I would find myself in a puddle of tears.

Annie didn't speak, she simply held me for a beat then released me to rush back inside. Thayer clapped me on the shoulder then went to stand on the side of the bride. Tash and Grace went to join the others as music from somewhere began to play.

"Get into place, Caesarion," Selene whispered, already standing underneath the arbor.

I was momentarily stunned by the swirling events but shook my head and went to stand to the left of Selene. As soon as I was in place, Jack ambled outside. I couldn't have been more surprised when he stood on my side of the white strip of silk. I wondered where Mills was.

The procession began. Grace came first, her smile so wide she melted every heart in front of her. The petals were scattered by huge handfuls as she walked. When she reached the end, she winked at me then went to stand alongside Jack.

Next came Annie in her velvet gown, looking like a sultry movie star. She held a tiny bouquet of red roses, her auburn hair lying around her shoulders in soft curls. Annie blew me a kiss as she stood to the right of Selene.

Millicent came next in a gown that matched Annie's. Mills looked every bit as beautiful as Annie in red, clutching the same red flowers. What surprised me to no end was that she didn't move to stand with Annie. Instead, she moved to the left, to stand with me.

The sentimentality was building, the dam about to break.

The wedding march began to play, and I took a deep breath. All eyes were on the back-terrace door as Tash stepped forward with Bria on his arm. Breathing seemed to be something I'd forgotten how to do. If Mills and Annie were my movie stars, Bria was my goddess.

Her flaming red hair fell around her in soft waves, dotted with tiny crystals that reflected in the candlelight. Bria wore a sleeveless white lace dress which, to my eyes, looked vintage. She looped one hand through Tash's arm and in the other held a large bouquet of red roses tied with a gold ribbon, the same color of Selene's dress. How Mills had managed all this, I would probably never figure out.

Bria and Tash walked down the aisle to the rhythm of the march. Bria's gaze trained on mine. When Tash released her to me and she took my hand, I broke.

CHAPTER TWENTY

Millicent

The ceremony was beautiful. When Alexandre took Bria's hand and he briefly wept, I too was overcome with emotion. I looked toward Annie, her lip trembling, then met the gaze of my love. A single blood tear slid from my eye. We were all exactly where we should be.

Alexandre had Bria, a wonderful, sharp-tongued woman who would keep him on his toes. Their child would be a bit of a wonder and I'd admit, I couldn't wait to meet the little baby when he or she came into the world. I did hope the happy couple would decide on immortality. Their child could always join them when it had grown.

Selene and Tash were also well suited. Selene, a strong, smart woman with an incredible history would bring joy to any man, but for Tash, she was perfect. He was also a man with a rich and storied past. Their affinity for vanquishing the world of evil beings would bring them many fulfilling years of hard work. And with a young lady like Grace at their side, anything was possible.

That Annie and Thayer were running off to join them didn't exactly thrill me. I so loved the time spent here at the chateau with my best friend and the man who was her ideal complement. These two had many traits in common; they were fearless, independent, courageous, but they were also different in a way that was almost comical. Thayer was stiff, serious, and his sense of humor needed work, while Annie was boisterous, funny, and the best time I'd ever known. These differences only brought them closer together. Without Annie, Thayer wouldn't be Thayer.

Then, there was my relationship. As much as I loved having these wonderful people under my roof, I wouldn't be terribly sad to see the house empty. I did enjoy quiet solitude, and solitude with Jack was my most favorite kind of peace. There would be an endless amount of love for us to share and no one else to interrupt us. I couldn't wait to get him squarely to myself.

After the ceremony, Thayer and Jack brought out the champagne and a small tray of food for Bria, Alexandre, and Grace. We stood in a circle, this strange group of incredible people, and toasted the future. Grace promptly went inside to sleep, her yawns becoming more and more pronounced.

Bria and Alexandre followed not soon after. As soon as the sun set on the next day, my friends would all be heading off to their new lives and adventures. Bria and Alexandre would go home to Ireland to await the birth of their child. The others would head to Russia to take on whatever lurked there, and Jack and I would find ourselves blissfully alone.

EPILOGUE

Millicent

The house was quiet. Jack and I hadn't known silence this deafening in some time. While Jack read, I pulled out my old eighteenth-century jewelry case. I wasn't looking for anything in particular. After my time spent in the past, I was in a nostalgic mood. I ran my fingers over Marie Antoinette's sapphire bracelet before clasping it on my wrist.

The jewels were as stunning today as they were then. I mused on what this object would be worth in today's market. Probably more than any of us possessed, although I would never part with it.

I took off the bracelet and laid it back on its velvet pillow. As I did so, I caught a glimpse of a folded-up piece of paper, the corner of which was sticking out of the back drawer of the case. After a couple of tugs, it came loose.

Imagine my shock to find a letter from Annie addressed to me at Chateau Mirabeau. The letter was written on paper now yellowed and brittle with age. The contents; a warning concerning Nephthys.

As far back into the past as I tried to strain my memories, I couldn't remember ever receiving this.

Strange how it reached me through time and alternate dimensions. I refolded the note, slipping it right back where it came from. The past had its place and I was no longer afraid of it.

DARK STAR

AUTHOR'S NOTE

Dear Readers,

I can't thank you enough for taking this ride with me. This series has fulfilled a life-long dream – to write my own vampire series with characters from diverse walks of life. It's been a pleasure to not only develop these voices, but to explore each unique past life and how those experiences shaped the immortals they became.

When I began writing Deepest Midnight, I had no plans to continue the story with a series. That book was meant to be a stand-alone. Instead, I found there was a world of stories in these characters that were begging to be told. I hope I've done them justice.

It was with a heavy heart that I finished Dark Star. I cannot say equivocally that these stories are over. You never know what the future will hold, but I can say that they are over, for now, and Dark Star feels like a fitting end.

I wouldn't have been able to do this without the fantastic support of Melissa Keir and Inkspell Publishing. Thank you so much for believing in these books. Thank you, Audrey Bobak, for your excellent editing eye, and Maria Spada for your spectacular cover designs, you captured the essence of every story.

Thank you to my family and friends for your love and support, especially my husband of twenty years, Brian, and my son, Quinn. I couldn't do this without you.

XOXO,
Clara

BOOK ONE OF THE IMMORTAL KINDRED SERIES

True love never dies.

For Millicent, a once French noblewoman turned immortal vampire, forever is a long time to live in despair. The love of her life is murdered the night she becomes immortal. Millicent spends her endless night in a melancholy which never ends. Two hundred forty years later, she locks eyes with an English actor, who happens to look exactly like her long dead love.

Sadness turns to happiness as Millicent and Jack find passion in each other's arms. Their fling quickly turns serious as Millicent finds happiness once again— and possibly her one true love.

However, their relationship becomes complicated by her own uncertainty, Jack's mortality, and the other man in Millicent's life, Alexandre, her maker and companion. When Alexandre puts his foot down, Millicent must decide if she's going to continue to be led by others or take the reins and drive the outcome of her life.

Deepest Midnight is set in modern day Savannah, Ga with occasional glimpses back to 18th century France. This is the first book in The Immortal Kindred Series.

Available at all major book retailers

BOOK TWO OF THE IMMORTAL KINDRED SERIES

Always and Forever

Annie is a Culper Spy captured by Hessian soldiers. Powerful and mysterious Captain Thayer Emmerich takes mercy and releases her. Annie is inexplicably drawn to the handsome German, but she hates the feeling of powerlessness the enemy has left her with. Annie would give anything to be stronger.

One evening at the famous Green Dragon Tavern, Annie befriends the ethereal Millicent. Soon after meeting Millicent, Annie discovers her secret--her new friend isn't human. Millicent introduces Annie to her maker, Alexandre, and Annie joins their preternatural family.

Annie finally has the strength and freedom she

needs to aid the revolution and see Thayer, once again. The two discover a passion neither has known before. But, too many complications exist for the pair to find happily ever after. Not only are they fighting on opposite sides of the war, the evil Emilia Romanov has plans for Thayer that do not include a love affair.

Rebel Heart is set in 18th century Boston and Savannah, as well as modern day Germany and France. This is the second book in The Immortal Kindred Series.

Available at all major book retailers

BOOK THREE OF THE IMMORTAL KINDRED SERIES

Love has no limits...

Alexandre has retreated from the world. He has no one to love, nowhere to call home. While licking his wounds in the middle of nowhere, Alexandre is approached by Irish lass, Bria. She has a proposal for him; to follow her to Ireland and fight demons.

Alexandre finds this amusing, but intriguing. More than anything, he is curious to see the individual who sent Bria, someone from his ancient past.

In Ireland, Alexandre confronts a dilemma greater than fighting demons. He must face down fiends of all kinds, deciding once and for all who he really is. Sparks fly between Bria and Alexandre, adding to the already complicated situation. Can a bad boy vampire really change?

The King of Kings is set in southern Ireland with a glimpse back to Ancient Egypt.

Available at all major book retailers

BOOK FOUR OF THE IMMORTAL KINDRED SERIES

An impossible attraction. An apocalyptic threat.

After vanquishing a Celtic death demon, Selene should be kicking back and enjoying some free time. However, her life is anything but relaxed. She must travel to Romania, the last place she'd ever thought she'd be, facing another demon threat. Just another day at the office for the daughter of Cleopatra.

The situation soon escalates. The simple problem Selene thought she was facing, becomes intense--FAST. The dilemma is much greater than she initially feared. Throw in a sexy witch she doesn't want to be attracted to, and her life really gets complicated.

Overconfidence leads Selene to make a mistake which could cost everything. Can she unravel the mystery before it's too late? Or will her latest nemesis be the death of her and those she loves?

Goddess of the Moon is the fourth book of The Immortal Kindred Series and is set primarily in Brasov, Romania.

Available at all major book retailers

ABOUT THE AUTHOR

A.D. Brazeau is an award-winning author who writes what she loves. From dark and fantastical fairytale retellings to quirky romance, and everything in between, she loves nothing more than to immerse herself in new worlds. A.D. Brazeau is a book-obsessed wife, mother, and dog lover, who grew up surrounded by stories. Not much has changed. A.D. is from Colorado Springs, Co, and currently resides in Orange County, Ca.